RELEASING MALADEK

A CLECANIAN SERIES NOVELLA

First paperback edition March 2023

Cover design by Mayhem Cover Creations

ISBN 978-1-958397-04-6

www.victoriaaveline.com

RELEASING MALADEK

A CLECANIAN SERIES NOVELLA

USA TODAY BESTSELLING AUTHOR

VICTORIA AVELINE

1

∾

Katie trailed behind Prince Skendro Mistra Endrolfen XV and scrutinized the thousands of colorful threads and chains that hung from his elaborate outfit. Neon lime, pink, and orange fringe swayed gently in time with his regal gait. When he swiveled to survey the ornate decor of the room, a few threads caught and tangled. Katie held back a frown. Out of all the outfits the prince had brought on the Myradium Galaxy cruise, this one was, by far, the most difficult to keep immaculate.

At first, when the staffing head of the Endrolfen palace had asked her whether she wanted to be a part of the small group of servants accompanying the prince on his cruise, she'd jumped at the opportunity. But her assignment turned out to be as dull as mud. Every day after Prince Skendro's personal maid helped him dress, Katie would follow the prince around, straightening any rumpled fabric, brushing out the long eyebrow feathers that swooped along the sides of his face, and generally making sure he looked as if he never moved, spoke, or ate.

Murmurs broke out, tearing her attention away from yet another tangle forming on the prince's slender shoulder. Dressed in finery that Katie was afraid to even brush against, aliens of all kinds meandered through the large room. As usual, she scanned each person until she came to an inevitable conclusion once again. No other humans.

She shouldn't be surprised. Katie was used to being the only human in the room. Heck, she was used to being the only human on the planet. She hadn't seen another of her species for over a decade now, and she doubted she ever would.

A group of dissatisfied guests holding fluorescent drinks caught her eye. They were glaring at the prince. Katie didn't blame them for their irritation. King Endrolfen had invited a small number of guests from Alliance planets across the universe to join the journey. Yet, not three days after boarding the new luxury cruise ship the king had commissioned, the prince decided the trip through the outer edges of the galaxy was uninteresting and demanded he be returned home.

Did it matter to him that every other guest aboard the cruise's maiden voyage didn't want to cut their trips short? She was unsure it even registered.

It's not that the prince was an uncaring person; he just didn't notice certain things. He'd been raised to ensure his planet ran smoothly. People he hadn't met personally were more like ideas to him, and he grouped them in his mind as such. Rarely, if ever, did he think about strangers as individuals with wants and needs that might oppose his own.

The prince paused in the center of the domed viewing chamber and stared up at a misty sea-foam green planet in the distance.

"What is that one called?" His melodic voice echoed around the room in the distinct way his species spoke. Not quite singing, but not speaking the way Katie did either. His voice reminded her of her cousin's cockatoo. But maybe that was just because Betuhinians, like the prince, all had bright feathers rather than hair.

Char Tomi, a Charkathan servant who was acting as a personal tour guide on the trip, stepped forward. He stared at the prince, a hazy pink mist swirling in his large black eyes as he telepathically answered the prince's question.

The curling pink vanished from Char Tomi's eyes and the prince huffed, his wide-set, fuzzy yellow brows turning down.

Katie shot a curious glance at Char Tomi as she rushed to smooth the knots in the long fringe of the prince's outfit.

The pink mist returned to his eyes, and his voice echoed in her head. *I reminded the prince that since he demanded a shortcut be taken, I have no record of what the sights along our new route will be. The crew is still scrambling to figure it out themselves.*

Katie raised her eyebrows at Char Tomi, exasperated.

"Perhaps next time, I'll try the Chedraken Galaxy cruise. Once my father succeeds in stationing one of his ships on each Class Three port, that is," Prince Skendro said as he peered around, bored.

Content all the fringe was perfect, Katie scanned the room. Establishing a new cruise line when there were already so many planets entrenched in the business was a vast undertaking, but she had no doubt King Endrolfen would succeed. The shining gold plating on every wall and the expensive sculptures that were changed out each night hinted at the amount of money he was willing to spend on this endeavor.

The luxurious furnishings of the ship, paired with the rare edge-of-Alliance border travel, would be a draw to many rich beings who were bored of their normal trips to the dying stars of Niath or the sun-drenched tropical planets in the Vamour Galaxy.

Katie had only ever been told about these popular tourist destinations. She was disappointed that her first trip off Betuhines would be over so soon.

In her mind, she tallied the credits she'd saved up over the years and reminded herself that if she really wanted to, she could take a vacation of her own. Go anywhere. See anything. A frown tugged at her lips. *All alone.* What good was seeing the universe if you had no one to share the experience with?

Char Tomi gave Katie a gentle nudge to get her attention, and she quickly caught up with the prince, already uninterested in the magnificent sight of space sprawling all around him.

Daydreaming might be okay at home, but it won't do today. Not with the frock our prince has chosen to wear. The dry humor in Char

Tomi's voice echoed through her mind, and she bit her lip to hold back her grin.

Unaware of their teasing, the prince settled onto a long chaise and waved his hand at Char Tomi. "A drink," Prince Skendro drawled.

With a quick nod, Char Tomi flashed out of sight. Katie remembered the first time she'd seen a member of Char Tomi's species do that. She'd been on a slaver ship, fifteen, alone, and terrified after having been abducted from Earth. Then this beautiful, tall, golden creature had appeared out of thin air.

Later, she'd learned their species simply moved more quickly than she was capable of seeing, but at the time, she'd thought it was magic. Then, when the woman had rescued her and brought her to the fairytale palace of the Endrolfen family, Katie decided the woman was more of a superhero.

Fifteen years later, she'd grown so used to the Charkathan's speed that she barely even flinched when they zoomed by her in the palace hallways.

In only a few moments, Char Tomi returned, holding a delicate, bulbous glass with fizzy black liquid. Char Tomi and Katie both waited in silence as the prince took a sip. There was a chance he'd be satisfied with the drink, but a larger chance that he'd ask for something else, though he would never pick anything specific, just force the servant to guess what he'd like in that moment.

After he'd taken a small taste and resumed looking lazily at the planet hovering in the distance, Katie and Char Tomi stepped back and relaxed against the wall behind his chaise.

"Would you ever go on a trip with me, Char Tomi?" Katie ventured, the pull to explore a new place tugging at her. He eyed the blond curl on her forehead that always popped free from her headdress and scrunched his wide mouth. She rolled her eyes and stuffed her hair under her cap once more. "As a friend, I mean."

The Charkathan found hair repellent, and Char Tomi had made sure to remind her on many occasions that her mass of wild blonde curls was unappealing. She, in return, would comment that the roughness of his thick golden skin was a bit too much like a rhino's for her liking. The insult always fell flat since Char Tomi had, of course, never seen a rhino.

I suppose. But only if you bring a hat. The gold hue of his skin warmed with a faint orange, hinting at his amusement.

Katie snorted, then quickly schooled her features when one of the prince's stoic guards side-eyed her.

Char Tomi had started working for the royal family not long after she had, and since he was the only other young person in the palace at the time, they'd been pushed to socialize more often than either of them would've liked.

At first, Char Tomi had found her curly hair and loud, clipped way of speaking grating. She'd found his constant, sudden voice in her head unnerving—to say nothing of the brutal honesty the Charkathan were known for.

Neither of them could recall when or how it'd happened, but they'd become friends. Their sour swipes about each other morphed into playful teasing, and they'd found themselves wanting to spend their free time together.

Char Tomi gave her a nudge while eyeing the prince, who'd just downed his drink. A small tangle had formed on his arm with the movement. Rushing forward, she smoothed it, then for good measure, used the comb stashed in the pocket of her gray, floor-length robe to brush out his eyebrows. As though he didn't even notice her, the prince's gaze remained fixed on the fog-covered planet in the distance.

"Are we getting closer to that bleak world?" the prince warbled. His gaze shifted to Katie suddenly, and she realized he was waiting for her response.

She studied the planet through the thick glass of the room. "It does—"

The answer died on her lips as the prince winced and held his hand up.

Gathering her thoughts, Katie reminded herself who she was talking to. The prince, along with all members of his species, were highly sensitive to sound. It was why they preferred the silent telepathy of the Charkathan so much.

Katie cleared her throat and softly sang her response in the way the prince liked. "It does look like it's closer, highness. Perhaps the crew have decided to show us a new sight on our way home."

The shadow of a wince still lingered on the prince's face, but he accepted her response as reasonable. He narrowed his eyes at the planet, his long eyebrow hair lifting at the corners as he scrunched his brow. "It's not much to look at, though. All gray clouds and—"

A sudden blaring echoed around the room, and Katie jumped, slapping her hands over her ears. Her frantic gaze landed on Prince Skendro. Surely if her head was pounding from the piercing sound, the prince's delicate hearing would be causing him crippling pain. But he appeared not to notice. His expression was serene and vacant, and he remained utterly still. Confusion took hold. Something was very, very wrong.

Katie spun toward Char Tomi. Her friend's wide black eyes were jumping around the room. She followed his gaze and found that many of the people who'd been wandering around the room and chatting now stood frozen in place with the same odd expression on their faces. Wait, no, not frozen. They were still moving a little. It was more like they were hypnotized, each of their relaxed postures identical. If she didn't know better, she'd think they were all listening to beautiful music rather than piercing screeches.

Those who weren't under a spell, like her and Char Tomi, were frightened and confused. One Fretelithian female was jarring her partner's shoulders with her bright pink tentacles, desperate to snap them out of their stupor.

Katie focused first on the people in the room who were moving, then the ones who remained still. Only certain species seemed affected by the noise. All the Betuhinians, the prince and his guards included, remained motionless with the same vacant expressions. The entranced guests numbered far more than those who were still cognizant.

"What's going on?" Katie yelled over the screeching.

Char Tomi's eyes swirled. *I have no idea.* His gaze shifted to the planet visible in the distance. *But we are much closer to that planet than we were a moment ago.*

The lights in the room flickered, and Katie's heart thrashed inside her chest.

I'll go check on the crew in the helm, Char Tomi said, before disappearing in a flash.

Katie felt the blood drain from her face as she stared at the spot where Char Tomi had stood a moment ago. This ship was run with a full Betuhinian crew. Her gaze drifted toward Prince Skendro and his vacant-eyed guards. *If the crew are all hypnotized too…*

Wiping her shaky palms on her robe and breathing deeply, she tucked a stray curl back into her headdress. The familiar action helped her to focus her thoughts.

She knelt in front of the prince and desperately crushed her hands over his ear holes. The fact that he didn't have external ears like hers, only smooth skin, and a small hole where his internal ear began ensured she was able to cover them easily, but it didn't seem to have any effect.

Katie's mind whirred. The urge to glance over her shoulder and see how much closer the planet had gotten caused her anxiety to spike and her mind to fog.

Char Tomi reappeared next to her. His skin had gone a pale shade of buttercream. He shook his head, and they stared at each other silently for a moment. There was no way to stop this ship.

With normal security measures in place and no way to communicate with the captain, it'd be impossible to get into the locked helm. Even if they could, they'd have a very slim chance of figuring out how to fly the massive vessel. Not with how fast they were nearing the planet, in any case.

The lifeboats, Char Tomi's voice choked out in her head.

Allowing herself to look at the planet, she gulped. They were close enough now to see breaks in the cloud layer.

Steeling her resolve, she rose from the ground and yelled at the top of her lungs. "We need to get to the lifeboats on the lower level. Everyone grab a…" She wasn't sure how to refer to the unconscious individuals. Calling them *the hypnotized* just seemed bizarre. "…person," she finished in a weak croak.

Some of the passengers sprang into action, but most remained frozen in place with horror-stricken expressions. Katie gripped Prince Skendro under the shoulders.

We won't be able to save them all, Char Tomi whispered inside her head, the pink mist in his eyes swirling in frantic circles.

"I know, but we have to try." A few passengers carried their own friends and loved ones behind her. Katie gritted her teeth as she dragged the prince through the doorway. His thin frame and nearly hollow bones made him lightweight, but he was quite tall and hard to maneuver, and the ridiculous tangled fringe of his outfit kept getting caught underfoot.

With a final glance toward the gray-blue planet, Char Tomi flashed away. Katie ignored the curdling in her gut. She could only hope his increased speed would be enough to get everyone aboard the lifeboats.

Shuffling backward, Katie dragged the prince through the ship and toward his family's lifeboat. Char Tomi flashed by, transporting more than thirty unconscious passengers in the time it took her to load the prince into his seat.

She activated the cryosleep gel bubble and watched as translucent blue sludge oozed out. It encased the prince's limp frame in a perfect, protective orb that would buffer any rough landing and keep its occupant unconscious until a habitable planet was found, regardless of how many years it took.

After she was sure he was secured, she moved to the other lifeboats, strapping in the unconscious passengers that Char Tomi continued to deposit and sending the boats out when they became full.

I've cleared the restaurants and the kitchens, Char Tomi shouted in her head as he finished loading a particularly large man into a seat next to his brother. *But it won't be enough if we can't get into the suites.*

Katie ran through the hours of pre-launch safety training she'd been subjected to as a companion of the prince. "We need to find a deck officer."

Understanding dawned on Char Tomi's face as he swiveled toward the manual emergency override that required a high-ranking crewmember's handprint. With a nod, he was gone.

Out of breath, her skull throbbing from the continual shrieking blasting from the speakers and her headdress hanging on by only a few pins, Katie raced to help the passengers streaming into the large bay.

She'd just finished activating the cryosleep orbs for a family of three when Char Tomi reappeared, lugging an unresponsive crew member with him. "Over there!" She pointed toward a glass case housing emergency override controls as she slammed her fist against a lifeboat release. The secured family shot away from the ship and sped toward the mysterious planet.

They still had time. Since this was the cruise's trial voyage, King Endrolfen had chosen to only allow half capacity to make sure everything ran as smoothly as possible and was up to his incredibly lofty standards.

If the king were here right now, she might kiss him for being such a cautious perfectionist.

Char Tomi succeeded in stretching the unconscious crew member's hand toward the emergency override and flashing red arrows suddenly pulsed on the ground of the emergency bay. The arrows branched off down every hallway, forming a path that ended directly below Katie's feet. A loud voice blared over the speakers, clashing with the continual piercing screech that had the passengers entranced. "Emergency override engaged. Please stay calm and follow the arrows to the lifeboats. Entry into atmosphere: twenty minutes. Evacuate. Evacuate. Evacuate. Emergency override engaged. Please stay…"

The urgent voice continued to repeat its message. Katie attempted to tune it out.

Scanning the area for someone to assist, she found others glancing around to do the same. It was inspiring to witness that, for the most part, the passengers who were awake were racing back and forth to the emergency bay, risking their lives to gather unconscious strangers from around the ship rather than strapping in themselves and jetting away. Despite the terrible circumstances, emotion welled in Katie's throat, warming her soul.

Satisfied that the folks nearby had things under control, she sprinted toward the port side of the ship. She dashed into suite after suite, the doors having been unlocked when the override was activated.

In the fifth room, Katie found a young woman tugging at the arm of her hypnotized partner, tears streaming down her face. Katie grabbed his other arm, and together they dragged the heavily muscled man through the ship and into a lifeboat.

With rasping, heaving breaths, Katie ran back toward the suites, a few others following behind her.

"Entry into atmosphere: twelve minutes."

This would be her last trip. They were out of time.

In the distance, she spotted the recognizable flash of Char Tomi dashing in and out of rooms. Occasionally, a rush of air would buffet her, telling her he was carrying someone to safety.

They cleared the last few people from the remaining suites and rushed back to the mostly empty emergency bay. Char Tomi stood hunched over with his head between his legs, wheezing. His skin had flushed to a fiery shade she'd never seen before. Sudden, cold worry consumed her. Though faster than lightning and quite strong, her friend could only run so much before he hyperventilated or his body quit on him.

"Entry into atmosphere: three minutes."

"We're out of time," Katie panted, dragging Char Tomi to the lifeboat where the prince sat, still unconscious.

Her friend nodded, not even having enough energy to project a response into her mind. He stumbled into the royal lifeboat and collapsed into a seat. Katie lingered at the entrance. She didn't spot anyone left in the emergency bay and hoped to both the Earth god as well as the Betuhines' gods that everyone on board had gotten away safely.

She stepped inside, her hand lingering over the release that would send their boat shooting away from the ship, when a strangled cry reached her ears. Her eyes flashed to the bay, and she saw an elderly man struggling to drag two individuals behind him. His steps faltered, and he scrambled to stand. He strained with all his might, but only managed to slide his friends a few feet.

Katie, no! Absolutely— Char Tomi didn't have time to finish his sentence or unbuckle his belt before she reached over and activated his cryosleep orb. Fury and hurt crossed over his expression a moment before the gel slipped onto his body and his eyes fluttered closed.

"I'll be right behind you," she whispered.

"Entry into atmosphere: Two minutes."

Adrenaline dulling her terror and narrowing her focus, she dashed out of the lifeboat, slapped the release, and flew toward the struggling man. With their combined strength, they were able to get both entranced people situated in a three-person lifeboat just as the ship's voice began to count down the seconds until the massive cruise ship would hit the atmosphere and likely break apart at the accelerated speed.

"Thirty, twenty-nine, twenty-eight…"

Katie just made out a croaky "thank you!" from the elderly male as she sped to activate the release, then barreled to a waiting lifeboat. Her sweaty hands fumbled with the smooth metal seat buckles, but she finally got them to lock.

"Ten, nine, eight, seven…"

She slammed her fist against the release and felt her stomach lurch as the boat careened away. Her hand was millimeters from the cryosleep button, when something large and heavy crashed into her and sent the lifeboat whirling through the air. Her body was rammed back and forth against her seat belt as she tumbled wildly through the atmosphere. She needed to get the gel activated soon, or she'd never survive the landing.

Tensing her limbs against the G forces threatening to pull her apart, she finally knocked the cryosleep button with her elbow. Before she could discern the feel of the blue gel on her skin, everything faded to black.

2

Maladek's body seized as the crude electrical current speared out from his collar and shot fire through his veins. When the sizzling pain ceased and he could breathe again, he let out a deadly growl and glared at the grinning Sieliji guard who took pleasure in *correcting* his behavior.

"Speed it up, grunt," the guard said in his piercing, discordant voice.

Violence sparked inside Maladek; he curled his fists and tensed his muscles. "Have a wish to be buried alive, *dreg*?" he shot back with a snap of his teeth.

The dimly lit mine the Sieliji had forced him to excavate for the past month was stable for now, but if this pishot guard with a penchant for pain and control didn't start listening to him, the glassy black rock overhead would fracture and crush them both.

Pale wet eyes flashing with cold fury, the Sieliji slammed one webbed finger onto a button at his hip and grinned as Maladek convulsed in time with the electricity pulsing off his collar.

It took every ounce of willpower he had to keep himself from lunging when the charge rattling his bones stopped. He'd made the mistake of attacking his captors too many times over the last month. All this Sieliji scum had to do was open his mouth and his hypnotic song would stop Maladek in his tracks anywhere within earshot.

Though it always felt good when he managed to land a blow, being hypnotized and waking up in a different place with no memory of what had happened or what they'd made him do was worse than quietly gritting his teeth and biding his time. Not when he was so close to escaping.

A chirp sounded from the guard's knotted belt. He glanced at the scrolling script running over the ancient communicator that was at least four decades out of date. Maladek gave his collar a covert nudge. He hissed softly as his blistered skin tore with the movement.

Though the collars were produced and maintained more often than most technology on this forsaken planet, the devices were still primitive. All the tech here was, since every piece of machinery had been scavenged from one crashed spacecraft or another for generations.

Not in the mood to be shocked again, Maladek pounded his fist into a fracture in the rock with a precise jab. A large piece of sharp black stone broke off cleanly, and he hauled it away.

"Drop that," the guard commanded, holstering his communicator. "We're leaving."

"I thought you wanted me to work faster," he grunted. The guard impatiently cleared his throat and Maladek swore, knowing what was coming next. Before he had a chance to throw the boulder to the side, the Sieliji's song began and a cloudy dream state wiped out all recognition of reality.

Warm and comforting, Maladek floated through memories of his home city, unaware the Sieliji had walked him all the way back to his damp cell until the cheerful visions were ripped away and frigid metal walls replaced the fire-warmed stone and crystal caverns of his mountain. When his mind cleared, he was alone, staring through the thick bars of his prison.

More than the insults or the torture or the work, Maladek hated being entranced. To be convinced he was home and happy for a moment, only for it to be ripped away over and over again was something a being could only stand for so long before their mind fractured. The Sieliji knew this.

Though their natural instinct was to entrance, they'd grudgingly resorted to using shock collars and threats more often than not. For a race of dregs unwilling and unable to leave their home planet, slaves were difficult to come by. Keeping them alive and working for as long as possible was paramount. It was a sore loss when a prisoner's mind broke, though their body would've been capable of work for years to come.

So why had the Sieliji entranced him then? And why bring him back to his cell this early in the day when he normally forced Maladek to work well into the afternoon?

Not just me. It seemed all the prisoners were being brought back to their cells. He watched from below as Sieliji captors walked their charges through the different tiers of the craggy, dried-up sea trench they'd developed into a rough prison.

Some of the enclosures on the highest tier before ground level were simple holes carved in the sandstone, flimsy metal grates slapped over their entrances. The weakest prisoners were kept in those cells. Down into the trench the cells became sturdier, as did the beings they contained, until the lowest level. The damp, dark, frigid base would fill up with water first if the Sieliji guards chose to open the dam at the edge of the trench in the case of a riot.

It was on this treacherous level where they'd placed Maladek. No crumbly sandstone or malleable metal were present in *his* cell. The walls were lined with askait metal a foot thick. The bars were made of the same material and as broad as his forearm, which was saying something considering his kind were built by the goddess to move mountains.

He couldn't blame the Sieliji for deciding to throw him down here. They'd witnessed firsthand what he was capable of. Perhaps if he hadn't showcased his strength in the battle that had stranded him on this planet in the first place, they would've stowed him higher up. Escape would've been all too easy then.

If his bars were even a half inch thinner, Maladek could have bent them. As it was, they only creaked and groaned no matter how hard he tried to pull them apart.

A murky puddle on the ground in front of him caught his eye. The surface of the water shook, the vibration growing stronger and stronger. He craned his neck to peer at the sky through the cracked opening of the trench. Suddenly, a wailing roar bounced off the walls as a fiery behemoth of a ship came into view. It hurtled across the narrow view of sky he currently had, dropping bits of mangled white-hot metal into the prison. He jumped back as a twisted, glowing piece landed in front of his cell with a thunderous crack.

Maladek's blood ran cold. They'd lured a ship to the surface.

Hypnotizing unsuspecting spacecrafts passing by and forcing them to crash onto their planet was the particular kind of savagery the Sieliji were known for, and the reason they'd been banished from the Alliance in the first place. Maladek had been trapped here a month, but he'd been fortunate enough to not yet witness the terrible practice in action.

The whole trench quaked, and shouts echoed from the cells above him. The ship had hit the surface and now the Sieliji would descend like a scourge, capturing any lucky enough to survive and tearing apart the usable pieces of the ship that remained. Heartless scavengers.

Worse still, he'd be forced to help. For the first time, Maladek hoped they'd entrance him. He'd rather not recall the horrific sights waiting for him in the wreckage.

3

Why was it so hot in her room? Had she forgotten to leave the window open again? Katie tugged at her shirt collar and squirmed. Slowly, awareness crept in, and she realized she wasn't in her bed at all.

A voice drifted in the air, starting out faint but growing louder as something sticky slid off her body. "Please remain seated until help arrives. Standing too soon after cryosleep may cause dizziness, fainting, and nausea. Your lifeboat has landed safely. Please remain…"

The warning repeated over and over. By the third time, everything that had happened rushed back to Katie. Dread kept her immobilized and seated, unable to get up even if the thick, hardened gel hadn't made movement impossible while it slid away.

Katie blew out a shaky breath. To her left, only three feet from her head, a sizeable dent bowed the metal wall of the ship inward. Something large had collided with that side of her boat. With a gulp, she studied the crushed headrest of the seat under the indent. If she'd picked that seat instead, she'd be dead right now.

Her fingers trembled, both from her nerves and the cryogel, but she managed to unbuckle her belt. A wave of dizziness hit as she staggered to the exit. She missed the release for the door, her palm landing a few inches away, her vision not quite back to normal yet. On the second try, she hit it.

Heavy briny air invaded her nose and her lip curled. There was something sweet yet rotten in the humid breeze, the scent turning her stomach. She hung her head, breathing through her mouth and leaning against the wall for support until the nausea passed.

Her first glance of the planet brought on confusion. The surface itself was rather barren. Flat sand and pools of water stretched out for miles in every direction as if the tide had just gone out, leaving shallow puddles behind. But what didn't immediately register in her brain were the numerous broken pieces of metal littering the landscape as far as she could see.

Upon closer inspection, she realized they were fragments of spacecrafts. Was it the cruise ship?

There was no great epicenter where the bulk of the ship had crashed, only small bits scattered around. Could it have broken up *that* much upon entry into the atmosphere?

She stepped through the exit onto the damp sand and shuffled slowly around the perimeter of the lifeboat. The nearest hunk of metal glinted, catching her eye.

Foreboding lifted the hairs on her neck. The air froze in her lungs, acid crawling up her throat. That ship lay rusted, and half buried in sand. The ones next to it, too. These weren't sections of the Endrolfen vessel.

Black plumes of smoke came into view on the horizon as she reached the far side of the lifeboat. She'd bet her Sunday evening yuba tart that's where their cruise ship had landed.

Katie gulped, eyeing the husks of spacecrafts in varying states of decay which spotted the path toward the billowing sooty clouds.

The sound…

The hypnotic effect it'd had on the passengers…

They'd crashed smack dab in the middle of a spaceship graveyard. And no part of her believed it was a coincidence.

***

Despite the layers of cloth she'd torn off her robe and wrapped around her mouth, the acrid fumes of the smoldering cruise ship still invaded her throat. If she were to speak, she imagined her voice would come out raspy and cracked, but she couldn't be certain, as she hadn't uttered a word in days.

Since crawling out of her lifeboat into a nightmare, she'd carefully picked her way toward the remainder of the wreck. Along the way, she hadn't come across anyone else, though she'd found a few empty lifeboats all fully stocked with their emergency supplies.

Katie didn't understand where the passengers had gone or why they would've left without any food or water until she came across a group of creatures prying open the door of a lifeboat that had malfunctioned.

She dove for cover and hid amid some wreckage as soon as she spotted the unfamiliar aliens, then watched as they worked together to tear the door away. Once open, the same screeching noise from the cruise ship rang through the air, but this time, to her horror, the sound emanated from the beings.

During her time at the Endrolfen palace, Katie had met many alien species. Some looked like her in one way or another. Some resembled animals or insects she'd seen on Earth. And others still she couldn't even begin to describe, for no part of them was familiar.

These beings stood on two legs and were humanoid, but the similarities stopped there. The razor-sharp fins protruding from the sides of their faces and arms, along with their bulbous black eyes and slick mint-green skin, reminded Katie of an angler fish crossed with an eel.

Two passengers she didn't remember helping appeared to succumb to the terrible song. They staggered out of the lifeboat with vacant expressions and, as though unable to stop themselves, followed one of the singing fish people away.

A third survivor leapt out of the lifeboat and charged at the three beings who remained, their song having no effect on him. Her heart pounded as the man kicked and punched, struggling to break away from the three fish people. But when one of them jammed a long metallic pole into his back, the man seized and shook as though he'd been shocked.

While he struggled to rise from the sand, they slammed a metal collar around his neck, then stood back. The man hadn't taken one lumbering step before they activated the collar, zapped him, and forced him to his knees once more. Over and over, they waited for him to recover and attempt a weak escape before sending a jolt through his body until, finally, he glared up at them in defeat. He walked between them after that, his round chest rising and falling with frustration at the understanding there'd be no escape.

Silently, Katie followed.

She studied them that first day, getting closer by darting from one piece of wreckage to another like a pinball when she was sure they were far enough away. After a while, the wreckage ended, the sand smooth and clear of obstruction for miles ahead.

She watched helplessly from behind the last mangled piece of ship large enough to hide her from sight as they led the prisoners toward a small building on the edge of a trench. Only the top of the pit was visible, like a jagged gash sliced into the sand.

Rather than going into the building like she'd expected, they led the prisoners down into the trench. A few minutes later, the fish people emerged alone and slunk into the building. After the bright glow of the sun behind the dense cloud layer almost disappeared from the sky and the beings had not emerged, Katie scouted the surrounding wreckage for a safe place to sleep.

One ship that'd been ripped in two lay a bit further away from the building but had a small closet in a hard-to-reach corner just big enough for her to squeeze into.

With a sharp rock, she carved a hole into a crumbling, rusted part of the metal exterior wall so she could keep an eye on the small building and trench, then spent a sleepless night on edge and terrified.

Using the emergency supplies her lifeboat had stocked, she managed to keep herself fed and warm while cramped in the small space. She'd remained there for days, waiting and watching as the fish people emerged in the early morning and set out on their hunt. For the first two days, they brought back more survivors. On the third day, it seemed they'd gathered everyone they cared to. Instead of venturing out, a larger group of fish people appeared from the trench, leading a slew of prisoners toward the smoking cruise wreck.

Stiff and bleary-eyed, Katie emerged from her closet and trailed behind, hoping to catch sight of Char Tomi or the prince among the group. When they reached the crash site, the prisoners were put to work. Any part of the ship that had cooled and was in half decent shape was dismantled.

The fish people sang to some of the workers, forcing them to haul loads of partially charred electronics and equipment toward awaiting rolling barges. Others were allowed to work on their own without being hypnotized. As she took in their ratty clothing and grimy appearances, it dawned on her that they must've been survivors of another crash. An older crash. How long had it taken for those prisoners to concede to work without being hypnotized? She suspected the shock collars around their necks were incentive enough.

Katie followed the group of prisoners and guards back and forth for five days, hoping to catch sight of something that might help her come up with a plan, any plan. So far, she'd been unsuccessful. All she'd managed was to eat through some of her rations and get a solid idea of their schedule.

She huddled on the far-left side of the cruise ship today, as far away as she could manage while still being able to see the workers. It helped that her drab, grayish-blue robe and headdress were exactly the shade of the sand. She blended in well enough, and it didn't seem that the inhabitants of this planet were too concerned with stragglers anyway. There had to be more passengers out there who'd been knocked off course like she had, after all, but the fish people had stopped looking after only three days.

Maybe they assumed the enormous creatures that came out at night had eaten them. In the evening, after the fish people locked themselves in their small building and she returned to her cubby, she could hear the monsters' massive bodies grinding along as they slid over the sand, making terrible squealing growls. Katie had only caught a glimpse of one through the crack in her wall on the second night, and it'd been enough to keep her bolting awake at every little sound each night after.

In the morning, she'd awoken to find divots in the ground as wide as buses. It sent a shudder down her spine even now to imagine what the animals who left those tracks must look like. A giant snake, maybe. Or a worm.

Either way, she decided that those creatures must be the reason the guards always disappeared into that building and remained tucked inside until morning rather than watching over their prisoners through the night.

She ran her fingers through the damp, smooth sand as she watched the workers tear apart the once gleaming ship. Her breath froze as a tall, thin person was led over to an intact refrigeration unit in the distance. She squinted, leaning forward on the balls of her feet. He had the right build and the bright hue of his gold skin could be dulled under a layer of dirt, but she couldn't quite see well enough to know whether it was Char Tomi. Had he survived?

She hadn't seen him or the prince in the crew that had come to scavenge the wreck, but she refused to believe they were dead. For one thing, Char Tomi should've been fast enough to escape even if they'd had the upper hand and gotten the jump on him. The person in the distance turned to haul some scrap away, and she got a good look at them. Her shoulders slumped. Too broad. It was clear, even from this distance. Not Char Tomi.

Wiping her watery eyes for the millionth time, she sat back. What now?

The sun was well over halfway to the horizon. Once it got a little lower, the fish people would herd the prisoners back to the pit they kept them in and lock themselves in.

The trench was the only place she hadn't explored yet. The prisoners stayed there all night long. Maybe she could sneak down after the fish people left and before the large monsters came out for the night.

Katie wiped her palms on her knees. She'd had this thought before and ignored it. There was so much she didn't know. What if there were guards down there? What if there was an alarm system? What if she got to the edge of the trench, figured out she couldn't sneak around, but before she could dash back to her hideout, was eaten by an enormous worm?

And say she did find her friends. What then? Would she lead them back to her closet? It wasn't as if she had a ship ready to go as soon as she found them.

All these reasons and more were why she'd only waited and watched. But she couldn't do that forever. At some point, she had to take a risk.

The fish people shouted to each other, and she tensed. It was time to go back. Despite herself, her gaze swung to the heavy barges loaded with scrap.

A group of five or six workers lined up in front of one of the barges, hefted a rope and pulled, dragging it through the sand. But they were not what made her throat go even dryer than before. They weren't who she was waiting for.

It took a few more minutes, but finally a man came into view, just as he'd done each day before. She could only make out the barest details from where she hid, but even seeing the blurry outline of him sent an odd shiver through her body. He was huge, built like a truck with thick limbs and broad shoulders. She thought he might be a shade of gray or perhaps purple, though it was hard to tell. Horns, one long and one short, shot out from his forehead and angled slightly over his crown.

Alone, he positioned himself in front of the second barge and with a strength that made her lips part in awe, dragged it behind him, leaving deep wheel ruts in the sand. She watched him until he faded from sight on the horizon. What would it be like to have that kind of strength? And how could a person that strong still be a prisoner on this planet? Even with the fish people's shocking spears, she imagined it would've been quite the feat to take him down and slap a collar around his neck.

Katie was hit with a bout of queasiness. If a person like that couldn't escape the trench, then what hope could she possibly have of breaking her friend and her prince out?

4

Commotion from above echoed down to Maladek, and he creaked one lid open. Lying on the cold, damp ground, his legs and arms crossed, his hands pillowing his head, he wondered whether whatever had the prisoners agitated was worth rising for.

The murmuring increased. With a groan, he stretched his stiff body and got to his feet. Peering through the crisscross bars of his cell into the dark trench, he couldn't make out much of anything. A small, tiered path lined each level of the trench, which meant he could only see the cells on the tiers nearest his.

Nothing out of the ordinary stood out to him. There was no ship crashing to the ground. No deadly quallie looming overhead. The large native beasts that roamed the planet at night did not have a taste for non-aquatic meat and therefore paid little mind to the prisoners in the trench. Sieliji flesh was the delicacy they sought, but occasionally, if they felt threatened or were very hungry, they'd lower their standards and eat a prisoner.

Maladek was about to give up and return to his uncomfortable corner when a barely discernible scent hit his nose. A bright, sweet note so unlike the smells that lurked in the prison. He found himself pressing against the door to his cell, face tilted to the left. Muttering was coming from that direction, about two tiers up.

Something in Maladek's chest snapped, his mind and senses homing in on the scent. Suddenly, the smell was no longer faint. It became all-encompassing, wrapping around him like a blanket. Bumps lifted on his arms, and every cell in his body stirred.

A growl started up out of nowhere in his throat and he gripped the bars to ground himself in reality. Was this another one of the Sieliji's tricks?

His chest swelled, heat coursing through every muscle, vein, and fiber. The world burst into focus. He could see farther than he could before. The taste of the sour air on his tongue grew sharper. The cold breeze hitting his heated skin overwhelmed him. He shuddered.

Had he been poisoned? Was the hypnosis finally breaking his mind? All Maladek knew was that his gaze traveled against his will, following an invisible beacon through the trench. His body ached to get closer. Whatever magnetic force lurked up there terrified him as much as it muddled his mind with intense longing.

The tingling of his body extended down his forearms, and movement on his hands caught his eye. Slowly, as if something crawled beneath his skin, drawing from the underside, designs started appearing on his hands and wrists. They stretched and wound themselves around his fingers in bright purple curves.

It took his brain a moment to catch on, his mind still screaming at him to return his gaze to the mysterious presence, which he somehow knew had ventured further to the left. His fingers tightened around the bars and his eyes slowly lifted to the tier right above him.

His mate was here.

Somehow, in this awful place, his mate had appeared. And she was in the trench, walking around freely. He'd learned in school that ancient mates had sometimes been able to recognize one another upon first scenting them. Some only had to see their fated match for recognition to occur. But Maladek had never imagined such a thing might happen to him. And certainly not here.

Abrupt, overwhelming instinct took hold as the shock wore off. How had she ended up here? Who was she? And what was she doing out in the middle of the night when the quallie were roaming?

He had to get to her. Keep her safe. His heartbeat thrummed through his body, making him pulse with anxiety. He pulled at his bars again and was surprised when they creaked more loudly than they ever had before.

He'd heard when a Clecanian recognized their mate, they became…more. Stronger. Faster. Better able to protect their partner and offspring. But matehood had been nearly extinct on their planet for centuries until very recently, and he'd never actually talked to another person about how the change felt.

His eyes traced the spot where some newly ignited intuition told him she was. The return of matehood had all begun with the arrival of humans on Clecania. Did that mean she was human?

His frustration doubled with the knowledge that his mate was on the other side of these bars. Her sweet scent built in the heavy air, and other urges took hold. A low growl rumbled in his chest as his shaft stiffened.

***

Katie crept through the strange prison quickly, peering into each cell as she passed by and checked for traces of Char Tomi or the prince. Occasionally, she saw someone she recognized from the ship. A few prisoners noticed her too, but most remained asleep. Instead of waking up the passengers she recognized, she continued to rush forward, peeking in each of the cells for only a moment before moving on.

What would she say to them if she woke them up anyway? *I'll break you out.* She couldn't promise that. As it was, she could barely help herself. And the more people who saw her walk by, the louder the commotion of the trench would grow. What if the guards came out to see what was going on? She'd be thrown in a cell and end up in the same spot as everyone else.

A few of the prisoners who noticed her tried to talk to her, but she couldn't understand them. Her translator was updated with all Alliance species languages every few months. The fact that their words weren't being translated must mean they didn't belong to the Alliance.

She peered over the edge of the pathway, which ran in a rugged spiral toward the bottom of the trench. There weren't many cells left, and the inhabitants of each cell grew more and more ominous as she traveled downward. She couldn't imagine the likes of Char Tomi or the prince being placed with creatures like the spiked stone being who'd glared at her with a dull gray eye from the last cell she'd passed.

But whether her friends were down here or not didn't matter. She needed to stay in the trench all night, anyway. It was too risky to sneak back to her closet now, while those creatures might be roaming.

A slithery voice hissed at her from up ahead and some deep part of her recoiled, skin slicking with sweat. Knowing that voice did *not* belong to anyone she knew, she kept her gaze averted and darted past the gloomy cell.

She came to the floor of the trench and paused. To her right, a couple of cells lined a muddy walkway which disappeared around a corner. Their doors were open, the area empty. To her left stood a metal door and past it, a hallway leading into the side of the trench. Katie pulled at the barred door to the passageway, but it didn't budge.

Tears blurred her vision without warning, and she rested her forehead on the cold metal. Her throat tightened and ached with welling tears. She was one stubbed toe away from completely breaking down.

Wrenching the unmoving bars back and forth with gritted teeth did nothing but force a few tears to spill down her cheeks. Heaving in a deep breath, her chin wobbled. Hope was getting harder and harder to hang onto. What was the point of any of this? She was just one person. One human at that. She had no skills other than ensuring a fussy prince looked tidy and keeping a palace clean. What was she supposed to do here?

Memories of her abduction from Earth came back to her and made her knees weak. One morning in the middle of winter, she'd been out in the neighborhood quite against her will. Her parents had forced her to wake up an hour before she should have to shovel their elderly neighbor's driveway. She'd complained and pouted and did all the immature things a fifteen-year-old might do to get out of chores. But like always, she'd lost her bratty battle.

She could still feel the cold bitter air of the morning, her nose running instantly, her skin sweaty from shoveling, yet freezing to the touch. A scream had echoed from across the street, as she'd finished clearing Mrs. Burnes' driveway.

All it'd taken was one curious glance through her neighbor's window, and her life had changed forever. She'd seen the woman from across the street, Jenny, unconscious and dangling over the shoulder of a reptilian monster. Katie had frozen, her shovel clattering to the ground.

She'd wanted to scream. She'd begged herself to scream, but like something out of a nightmare, her voice had lodged in her chest. The creature's yellow eyes had met hers through the window, and without pause, it'd bounded toward her.

Tears had frozen in tracks down her cheeks as she'd remained stuck in place. The scream building in her throat had finally made its way to her lips when the creature sprayed her with something, and everything faded to black.

The helplessness she'd felt that morning and, for weeks after, was something that still haunted her. It was why she'd stayed at the Endrolfen palace so long after she was free to leave. There was safety in the palace. She had friends and a warm bed and some semblance of control.

Now look at me. Huddled at the bottom of a prison trench on a horrific planet, with no hope of finding her friends or getting home. Her breaths came in quick gasps, and she slammed both hands over her mouth to contain the sounds of her sobs, head pounding with the effort.

When she'd been wrung out, she allowed herself to sit for a few minutes more, somehow feeling worse and better at the same time.

No, she scolded herself. *You're stronger than this.* Yes, she'd been helpless. She'd been kidnapped and traded like an animal, but she'd also survived. She'd made a life for herself when she could've given up. Katie was stronger than she gave herself credit for in these moments of doubt, and she'd be damned if she gave up now.

There was still hope. And even if it was a feeble hope, what was the alternative? Shutting herself in her closet and using up her rations until they were gone, then wasting away?

Using the train of her headdress to wipe her tears, she patted her cheeks, tucked the curls that had broken free back under her cap, and straightened her robe. She threw her shoulders back. There had to be some way to get through this door. A few bits of metal were strewn across the ground. If she found one strong enough, maybe she could pry the door open.

She crept through the trench floor, avoiding the large puddles that had settled down here. It didn't seem like the fish people cared much for upkeep on the lowest level. As she passed each open, empty cell, she wondered if it was because there was nobody down here.

The cold of the shadowy trench leeched into her skin and made her shiver. Katie wrapped her arms around her waist and pushed herself to venture further into a section of the trench where the moonlight barely shone.

So far, there wasn't anything usable. Only thin pieces of scrap. Where was the crowbar-shaped trash when you needed it?

Rounding a shallow curve, she spotted a pile that looked promising. She'd taken two steps toward it when a rustling to her right made her freeze. Her gaze lifted and met intense, ruby red eyes.

Still crouched in place with one hand reaching toward the wreckage, she scanned the features she could make out in the dim light and sucked in a quick breath. It was the man. The strong one who dragged the barges back every day.

He stared at her, his massive palms gripping the thick bars. Her skin flushed, and a flutter started in her belly under his unblinking scrutiny.

She averted her gaze and forced herself to rummage through the scrap pile in front of her.

"What are you doing?"

Katie froze again, his deep, rasping voice making goosebumps erupt across her skin. Despite her mind urging her to ignore him, her head turned. She'd understood him, which meant he was speaking in an Alliance language.

"Come closer," he insisted when she just stared at him.

Despite everything in her brain screaming to run in the opposite direction, she found herself wanting to comply. His skin was covered in grime, his dark hair a tangled mess. But something about the structure of his face, the curve of his lips, and the heavy masculine set of his brows had her stomach dipping.

"Leave me alone," she breathed, her voice coming out shaky. She needed to snap herself out of this and leave. Not because she had anywhere important to be, but because this man was doing odd things to her.

"What's the harm in talking to me?" He flicked his bars with a thick forefinger and a ping echoed off the stone walls. "I can't bite you."

Can't. Not won't.

Katie swallowed and licked her lips. Heat rose in her cheeks when he tracked the movement of her tongue. "I'm looking for my friends," she croaked. Her voice was just as raw as she'd imagined it would be. Clearing her throat and lifting her chin, she donned a confidence she didn't feel. "Have you seen them? One is a Charkathan. He's tall and thin and gold. The other is Betuhinian. He's also tall and thin. Orange feathers."

The man's full lips firmed. "I have not."

She studied his cell. The top half had crisscrossing bars, the bottom half solid black metal. There was a large rectangular box with a hole, maybe some kind of keyhole, positioned in the center of his door. Five-foot sliding bolts ran across the front of his cell, secured to thick metal on either side and, though strong, it seemed they could simply be slid out of place by a person outside the cell.

Emboldened by the strength of his prison, Katie stepped forward. "Do you know where that tunnel leads?" She pointed in the direction of the locked passage door, though it was out of sight around a corner.

"I know a great deal about this planet. Let me out and I'll help you find your friends." His dark gaze was unblinking and eager.

Katie let out an incredulous chuckle. The absurdity of the request was clear to both of them. His nostrils flared in time with his deep, measured breaths and his jaw clenched.

She spun away and dug through the pile of scrap with more fervor.

"I can open that door," he urged. "And I know of other prisons where they might be holding your friends. The Charkathan would be a boon to them, but only if they could control him. I'd say they're making him work over in the sea mine."

Her heart leapt when a long pole came into view. She tugged at it, and it pulled free with a loud metal on metal scrape that set her teeth on edge. "Where is the sea mine?" she asked while examining her new tool.

The corner of his mouth lifted, his white, even teeth flashing into view. "Let me out and I'll show you."

She crossed her arms over her chest. "I can't let you out even if I wanted to. Your cell needs a key." She gestured to the large black box on his door, but his expression remained unmoved.

"All you need to do is slide the bolts out of place."

She eyed the lock. "I'm gonna have to pass."

His knuckles paled as his grip around the bars tightened. Reigning in his frustration, he argued, "I vow to help you if you let me out. I'm strong and a good fighter. You'll need me in case you run into trouble."

Katie chewed on her lip. "Why should I believe you?" And why was any part of her considering his offer? Shaking her head before he could answer, she held up a palm. "Wait. No. Never mind."

"You'll never get it open with that," he called as she strode away.

Three broken nails, one broken pipe, and innumerable uttered curses later, she returned to the scrap pile and dug for something else to use. Embarrassment at her failure ensured her blush was hot on her cheeks.

"Told you." His voice wasn't smug exactly, more straightforward, as though her impending failure had been a simple fact.

Her teeth ground together. She reached the bottom of the pile and found nothing else that could be of use. Katie wanted to hang her head, but she didn't want her onlooker to see.

"Will you release me now, little human?"

Like a shot, her head snapped around. Eyes wide, she stared at him. "How do you know I'm human?" She'd never met a human outside of Earth before. How could this man possibly know what she was just by looking at her?

He shrugged. "You look like a human."

She pursed her lips. "Okay, but how do you know what humans look like?"

With a thoughtful lift of his chin, he studied her. "Release one of my bolts and I'll tell you."

Katie frowned. Curiosity burned in her, forcing her to rise to her feet and scan the five long bolts keeping him trapped. They were an inch thick at least and four inches wide. What was the harm in releasing one? Surely even *he* couldn't get out with four holding him in place.

Her skin prickled as she passed his door and wrapped her palm around one of the bolt handles. She tugged at it, expecting the metal to slide easily, but it turned out to be heavier than she'd realized. Using her body weight, she threw herself back, slowly tugging the heavy bolt until it finally scraped free from the door.

When she took her place in front of his cell again, his blood-red gaze flashed toward a curl that had popped free from her headdress. His brows furrowed and his hands twitched.

She quickly tucked her hair back into place. "I did what you asked. How did you know I was human?"

His eyes remained fixed on the place where her frizzy curl had been before he slowly answered, "There are some humans living on my planet. I've met one and know of others."

Katie had to remind herself to breathe. Humans, plural? Her happiness was smothered by a dark thought. "Are they there freely?"

His mouth pulled into a scowl. "They didn't arrive that way, but once their captors were apprehended, they were given their freedom. Most live happily, I believe. I'm sure they'd prefer to be returned home, but—"

"It'd be against the law," Katie finished. His heavy brows drew together at that, his gaze curious, but he said nothing.

She'd struggled over whether to sneak back to Earth many times. One of the reasons she hadn't was because even getting near a Class Four planet such as Earth was illegal. It sounded like his home planet had punished the ones who'd kidnapped people from Earth, though. That had to count for something.

"So, you've really met another human? What were they like? What planet are you from?" A tendon in his neck firmed and his throat bobbed as she spoke. With a gasp, she realized in her excitement she'd stepped far too close to his cell. Before she could dash away, however, his hand shot out, grabbing her wrist.

A strangled cry lodged in her throat, and she froze, knees shaking.

"Calm. I won't hurt you, female." His voice was a low caress, and, despite the situation, she relaxed a fraction. His massive palm swamped her wrist, but his grip wasn't painful.

As their gazes met, black slowly crept out from the corners of his eyes and blanketed them until she could no longer see any white or his red irises. Just inky black. "I swear," he began, watching her with such a determined intensity that she couldn't help but hang on each word. "If you release me from here, I'll do everything in my power to help you find your people and get us all off this planet safely."

Holding her stare, he peeled his fingers off her wrist.

Katie took a step back and held her arm to her chest, touching the skin he'd warmed with his palm. She couldn't force herself to look away. He appeared serious. Deadly serious.

"You'll help me open that door?" Was she really considering this?

He gave a short nod. "If you wish."

"And you won't hurt me?"

A flash of anger lit his features. "No," he gritted out. When she still said nothing and made no move toward him, he uttered the very thought she'd been struggling with. "What other options do you have?"

That was the crux of her problem. Katie had *no* options. And now that she'd explored as much of the trench as she could, she was out of ideas. There was nowhere left to search other than the hallway she couldn't get into and the building that the fish people disappeared to every night. But trying to sneak in there alone, not knowing how many remained inside, was beyond idiotic.

She filled her lungs with a deep breath and stepped toward the bolts. One by one, she strained to pull them open. The man remained silent as she worked. When the last one was almost out of place, she paused, heart ramming against her ribs. Sweat slid down her spine. *This is a mistake,* her mind whispered. Before she could lose her nerve, she yanked the last bolt out of place, then warily backed away from the cell.

"Thank you," he rumbled.

She swallowed. "I still don't know how you plan on dealing with that lock."

He gave an ominous chuckle and stepped back into the darkness of his cell. A thunderous crash boomed all around her as he rammed into the door at full speed. The metal bowed.

Katie sped away until her back hit the wall of the trench while he threw himself against the cell door again.

This time, the gap between the door and the metal frame grew by an inch and a massive bolt came into view in the widening space. With one final ram at the door, the lock slipped free. Though the bolt was still secured in place, the center of the door was so badly mangled that it could no longer reach its home. The door groaned open.

Like a terrified rabbit, Katie's pulse vibrated through her. Palms slick, she balled her fists.

With slow, heavy steps, the man emerged from the cell, tipping his head so his one long horn cleared the doorway. When he was out, he straightened to his full height and Katie took in a shaky breath.

Why the hell did I let him out?

He must have been crouching to speak to her because he was even taller than she'd thought. Wider too. The darkness of his cell had concealed most of his body, but now, in the dim moonlight, she could make out every towering inch. His loose, torn clothing did nothing to disguise the layers upon layers of heavy muscle underneath.

She raised her gaze to his and held his stare. There was no going back. What would he do now that he was free?

Her inhale remained locked in her lungs as she waited for him to make a move. His onyx eyes practically glowed as his gaze trailed up and down her body. At her involuntary shiver, his attention snapped back to her face.

"All right," she managed to squeak out. "Why don't we go get that door open?" He remained as still as a statue. Katie swallowed again and forced herself to blink. "You promised," she reminded weakly.

His jaw tensed at that. When his dark expression grew stony and determined, Katie took a clumsy step to the side.

"You're not going to open that door, are you?" she breathed, already seeing the answer in his hollow frown.

A strangled whimper burst from her lips as, without uttering a word, he rushed her. In one smooth movement, he crouched, pushing his shoulder into her stomach and forcing her upper body to sprawl over his back.

5

Maladek's mate shrieked and pounded on his back, dragging her nails over every bit of his skin she could reach. Groaning inwardly, he raced around the trench path. He should have waited, explained, but his body and mind had revolted against it.

His mate was here within his grasp, and for the time being, unsafe. All he knew was he had to get her somewhere secure. Somewhere where he felt comfortable. A place he could control.

His strides were quicker than they'd ever been, the mating bond allowing him to run faster than normal. The angry shouts of prisoners echoing in their wake became a mere buzzing in his ears. The scent of his mate and the feel of her soft curves under the rough fabric of her robe occupied far too much space in his consciousness. Maladek shook his head, trying to clear his mind before venturing into the open stretch of sand above the trench.

All he'd wanted to do upon first seeing her was rage against his cell door until it no longer separated them. Thankfully, his rational mind had still had enough reason to understand that with the bolts in place, he'd never make it out.

He'd struggled to hold back the impulses thundering through him, and instead attempted to *convince* her to let him out of the cage. Demanding that she release him so he could bend her over the nearest boulder and ease the screaming pull of the new bond would not have gone over well.

But calming his tone enough to earn her trust had taken every ounce of willpower he'd had. As soon as he'd emerged, he'd been unable to hold back any longer. Once she was safe and he could take a moment to calm himself without worrying she'd run away, his reasonable side would return. He was sure of it.

But what would he do then? Tell her she was his mate, and he'd been unable to control himself? If her furious wailing was any indication, he'd bungled their first meeting. She was spitting mad, and he couldn't imagine she'd take kindly to the revelation that they were bonded for the rest of their lives. Resolve and greed hardened his doubts, and he let out a low breath. It didn't matter. She was his. In time, she'd forgive this misstep.

He paused at the top of the trench, peering out into the dark moonlit desert.

"Quiet, female, or you'll attract the quallie." It wouldn't take long for him to get to the hiding place he'd found a few days ago, but it would be infinitely harder if a quallie suddenly took a liking to them.

She didn't stop, though. The small human continued to screech at him like a moorshut lizard. Now that he had paused, no longer jostling her about on his shoulder while running, she was able to raise her upper body, reach her arm around, and scratch at his face.

Her nail scraped against his eye, and he snarled. Hiking her high until she fell over his shoulder once more, he tore two long pieces of fabric off the bottom of her robe.

Maladek made sure he tossed her off his shoulder with enough momentum that she remained unbalanced after landing on her feet. Then, he spun her around and wrapped a piece of fabric around her wrists, binding them at her back.

When her balance was restored and she realized what he was doing, she fought, slipping on the damp ground as she tried to run away. All her thrashing and squirming about was going to make this next part difficult. He pushed her forward until her front was plastered against the wall, then lifted a knee to her back, pinning her and freeing his hands. He slipped the other strip of fabric around her mouth and tied it in place.

She whirled on him as soon as he lowered his knee. An angry flush colored her skin, and she threw one foot out to kick him in the groin. He dodged her easily, nearly sighing at the show of her ferocious spirit. He tore his gaze away from her dazzling yet furious blue eyes and the yellow curl that had come loose from her bonnet once more.

When you get her somewhere safe, you can stare at her all you want. She could scream herself hoarse while he learned every curve of her face, but for now, he had to get her out of the open. Tossing her over his shoulder, he listened, and was relieved to hear that although she was still screaming at him, the sound was muffled.

He sprinted through the sand, his thighs burning at the sharp turns he had to take to avoid the deceptively deep puddles littering the ground. A flash of pale pink appeared ahead between some large pieces of wreckage, and his grip on her thighs tightened. He hadn't realized how much until she let out a sharp cry.

Darting behind a rusted spacecraft, he loosened his grip and lowered her from his shoulder. She struggled in his hold as he turned her about, her back pressed against his chest, and slammed a hand over her mouth. He angled her head in the direction of the slithering quallie and could tell the moment she caught sight of it because her yammering stopped, and her body stiffened.

It hadn't seemed to notice them yet, so he remained crouched with her snugly pressed against his chest as he waited for the quallie to continue on its way. He shouldn't be enjoying the feel of her wrapped in his arms quite as much as he was, not in this situation anyway, but an unbidden purr rose in his chest.

He held her in place long after he was sure the quallie had gone. When he lifted her back to his shoulder and set off, she remained silent.

A smooth, round opening in the sand appeared up ahead, and he sprinted for it. After months of excavating the mine under the watchful eye of his Sieliji guards, Maladek had finally sensed another tunnel nearby.

The black interior of the mine loomed ahead, calm and reassuring in its solid structure. Knowing that most beings didn't find the dark confines of the earth as relaxing as his people did, he grabbed a few portable lights left at the mine entrance.

The air was damp and heavy as he jogged deep into the mine toward the hidden spot where he'd sensed the other tunnel system, but at least it was warm. He ran his hand along the wall, tapping the hard plates of his knuckles on the stone until the vibrations grew thin.

His female glared at him in the soft lantern light as he set her on her feet.

"Don't run," he warned, meeting her furious stare. "You won't get far, and you saw what's out there." He held her glower for a few moments. Satisfied she was smart enough not to chance a meeting with a quallie, Maladek set to work.

*** *** ***

Katie was livid. And confused. And to her utter exasperation…impressed.

She watched as the no-good, lying scumbag used his bare hands to pound through the sharp stone wall. What was he thinking? Had he carried her away just to show her how good he was at punching rock?

At least it's warmer down here, Katie mused while turning in place. Her shoulders curled forward as she studied the looming darkness pressing in on all sides. A sudden strange fear that an animal would come barreling out of the pitch-black tunnel forced her to step closer to her captor.

An echo louder than the rest suddenly boomed through the space, and she spun. All she could make out at first was the smug curl of the man's lips while he stared at the side of a wall. When she took a few more steps to the right, though, a new passage came into view.

"How did you do that?" Katie said, or rather, tried to say through the fabric in her mouth. All that came out was a muffled jumble of sounds. Anger that he'd tied her up in the first place rebounded, and she glared at him. Her arms were stiff from being restrained behind her, and the corners of her mouth were sore from the rough fabric pulling at her cheeks.

So what if he could carve optical illusion passageways out of volcanic rock? He was still a dishonest savage who'd carried her off for who knew what reason.

Eyes no longer black, he narrowed his red gaze at her and wrapped a meaty palm around her bicep. He guided her through the cramped opening in the rock, then pushed his shoulder through. The fit was so snug that for a moment, she wondered if he'd get stuck. Unfortunately, he didn't, but a sharp bit of stone did gouge his shirt. The fabric split diagonally across his chest as he squeezed through, exposing smooth, defined muscle under the torn halves.

It was harder than she would've liked to tear her gaze away.

Lifting the light, he scanned the perfectly round tunnel in both directions. Dripping water echoed from somewhere unseen, but the tunnel was otherwise silent. Disturbingly so.

Finally, the man lowered the light and let out a relieved breath. "We'll be safe now," he said, nodding at her as though agreeing with his own statement.

A muscle twitched in his jaw when she only glared at him. He took a step toward her, and she leapt away. His shoulders shot back in time with his soft growl. "Would you like to remain tied up, then?"

Katie had the odd urge to nod. His exasperated tone was just so irritating, as if *she* were the unreasonable one here. But remaining bound just to spite him was stupid. Tilting her chin up while giving him an imperious glare, she spun, presenting her hands to him. Though she knew it was coming, she jumped when his warm fingers brushed over her skin. His hands lingered on her wrists, squeezing gently after the fabric had fallen away.

His rough, strong palms felt so good rubbing her sore wrists. Too good. With an angry tug, she pulled her arms out of his reach. She'd be damned if her touch-starved body allowed this man any leeway after what he'd just done.

Pulling at the fabric around her mouth, she took a few more steps away from him. She stretched her chin, opening and closing her mouth when the gag was finally gone.

Before she could lose her nerve, she sucked in an angry breath and readied to shout all the foul curses she knew at him.

"You vile, lying heathen!" The words were dull as they spurted out of her mouth. What was she, a Victorian era grandmother?

The man remained unmoving before her, but raised a brow at her insults. Katie wanted to stomp her foot in frustration. She'd been young when she'd been taken from Earth, and though she'd heard other kids in school use curse words, she'd always been too nervous to use them herself. Then, after she'd been abducted, improper language at the palace had always been looked down upon. Even the Charkathan, who could say whatever they wanted inside each other's heads, rarely, if ever, cursed.

Still, if anyone deserved a tongue lashing, it was this man. "You're a…a…fucker!" Her cheeks heated, undercutting the tone she was going for. "You screeching manifti!" she added, trying an insult she'd heard the Charkathan use.

Both of his brows lifted at that. *Great.* She couldn't even offend someone correctly. Tears sprung to her eyes.

"You promised you'd help me," she breathed out shakily. "You lied." It was a stupid, useless thing to say, yet she couldn't help but feel betrayed by this stranger.

"I didn't lie," he finally rumbled, stepping toward her. She hurried away, stumbling on a ragged strip of her robe that he'd left dangling when he'd torn it. He stopped in place, but his big body was strung tight, his muscles clenching and unclenching as if he wanted to pursue her.

"Then what is this?" she cried, throwing her hands around the space. "You said you'd help me open that door. You said you'd help me find my friends. You said you'd keep me safe, and yet the first thing you did was run into the desert where those monsters are."

His eyes tracked a tear as it spilled down her cheek, and he looked as if he were being stabbed in the gut. Katie couldn't make sense of him.

"I'll help you do all those things." His voice was low and sure. "I'll open that door if you wish. I'll find your friends. I'll do anything you ask me to do. When you…when I recognized…" He sucked in a massive breath and scrubbed a hand over the back of his neck. "It's hard to explain, but I just had to get you somewhere safe first."

She stared at him, mouth open and brows scrunched. Confusion muddled her frustration and anger. "We were safe there," she argued, her tone pitched higher than normal. "Those people don't come out until the morning and those worm things don't go into the trench."

He peered around the dark tunnel as if looking for a good explanation. Finally, he shrugged. "I'm more comfortable here."

"You're more comfortable here?" she repeated, a sharp edge to her voice. "You threw me over your shoulder, ran straight toward danger without any supplies, any food, any water, to this random cave, because you wanted to keep me safe, and you *prefer* it here?"

When he did nothing but hike his enormous shoulders, Katie let out an incredulous squeak of laughter. She paced in a circle, fiddling with the pins of her headdress. What was she supposed to say to that? He appeared calmer and hadn't made any move to toss her around now that they were alone and stationary.

When she turned back to him, his eyes caught on some of her hair that'd poked free. He gazed at it with such burning intensity that she felt naked. Quickly, she tucked the hair back into place. She was about to re-secure the pins, but before she could manage it, he'd crossed to her and, as if unable to help himself, gently tugged the fabric away.

"Hey!" she barked, as the few remaining pins holding her hair in place were pulled free with a pinch. He dropped the headdress to the ground and took her face in both of his big palms.

Katie couldn't seem to breathe as he buried his fingers in the curls at her neck, tilting her head this way and that. He gazed at the rumpled mess of her hair with wide eyes and a soft smile, as if it were the most beautiful thing he'd ever seen.

His fingers dug into her curls, arched and scratched across her skin. Despite her situation and despite how confused she was by this man, her lids fluttered at the feel of his deft fingers kneading her scalp.

Katie hooked her hands over his wrists, fully intending to pull away, but instead had to focus all her energy on keeping the moan building in her throat from escaping. A delightful shiver ran down her spine as he leaned far too close, burying his nose in the hair at her temple and inhaling deeply.

She was so used to hiding her hair in public and rarely, if ever, was she touched. Not like this. Not by a man who, by his own account, had been so overcome with fear for her safety that he'd acted like a caveman without thinking.

When his long exhale brushed hot air over her ear, Katie failed to stifle a clipped sigh. The man pulled away. His gaze shot down to her. As if realizing where he was and what he was doing, he let his hands fall.

Though the tunnel they currently occupied was by no means cold, Katie felt a chill when he took a few steps away from her. His throat bobbed and his fingers twitched as he eyed her.

"Don't do that again." Pushing that sentence out of her mouth was like pulling teeth. For some reason, she very much wanted him to do that again. "You need to take me back to that door. I have to see if my friends are there."

The man's mouth hardened. "I'll help you look, but I will not return you to the trench. They aren't behind that door."

And just like that, the gentle buzz that his mini scalp massage had caused faded away. "How do you know?"

"Because that door leads to a secondary control panel for the dam. No one is kept there."

Katie's fingers curled, and she ground her teeth. "If you knew that, then why didn't you say something?"

He hiked his shoulders. "I needed to convince you to release me from the cell. If I'd told you there was nothing behind that door, you wouldn't have needed me for anything."

While that wasn't entirely true, she begrudgingly saw his point. "So, do you have any idea where they are? The sea mine? Or were you lying about that, too?"

A muscle flexed in his neck. "What I said is true. They could be in the sea mine. But I will not be taking you there. It's too dangerous."

She placed her hands on her hips. Katie was getting annoyed with this whole *danger* shtick. "What happened to *I'll do anything you ask me to do?* So far, you've refused to help me do anything at all. You've brought me to an empty tunnel underground without any of my supplies. What are—"

"Your supplies?" The man lifted his immense hands to his own hips, mirroring her stance.

"Blankets. Food. Water. Medicine. The emergency bags from the lifeboats on our ship have everything. I left two of them in the place I was sleeping. Now, we don't have anything."

His gaze lit at her words, his shoulders lifting. "They're in all the life pods that fell?"

"Yes, but—" Katie raised her hands as he backed away from her. He began squeezing back through their tunnel entrance. "You can't go out now! You just got through telling me how dangerous it was."

"I'll bring you back everything you need to make up for my behavior."

Katie sputtered. "No, you can't... I didn't mean you should go charging out in the middle of the night."

His head dipped to peer at her through the craggy opening. "Before I leave, will you tell me your name?"

The image of the gigantic worm creature she'd seen on the way here flashed through her mind, and her pulse pounded in her ears. What if he got killed trying to get her bags? "Stay. We can get them tomorrow."

He didn't respond, just kept his brows lifted, waiting for her name. With an exasperated sigh, she dropped her hands. "Katie," she answered. "What's yours?"

"Maladek." His eyes ran over her face, appreciation clear in his drawn brows. "I will win back your trust, Katie." With that, he disappeared.

6

Katie huddled against the far wall, staring at the dim opening of the tunnel. She'd paced back and forth for a few minutes after he'd left, using the lantern to study the glossy black walls. It looked like some kind of volcanic rock. She ran her thumb over it and pulled back with a hiss of pain. It was sharp like volcanic rock, too. She once again marveled that he'd been able to carve through it with his bare hands.

For a moment, she pondered whether she should try to hack off a slice to use as a weapon, but decided against it. She didn't have anything to break it with and she'd probably only end up hurting herself if she tried. Also, for some reason, she didn't feel she needed it.

Katie knew she should be terrified of Maladek returning. She should be searching for another tunnel or risking a sprint through the desert to find a new hiding spot. But the only thing that worried her was that he wouldn't return. For the life of her, she couldn't understand why she wasn't more afraid.

Annoyed? Yes. Angry? Yes. Intrigued? Unfortunately, yes. But not scared.

He'd seemed so sheepish when she'd criticized him for bringing them both here. It was like he knew it'd been an impulsive thing to do and was embarrassed. Katie couldn't pinpoint why exactly, but she got the sense that he didn't feel he'd had a choice in the matter. She'd gotten the same feeling when he'd touched her hair. Like he just couldn't help himself. But what sense did that make?

She had no idea how much time had passed when noise echoed from outside the tunnel and she spotted one long horn and one short one peek through the opening. Now that she had a moment to study his horns as he attempted to squeeze his bulk into the tunnel, she realized that his shorter horn ended in a precise, flat surface—as though it'd been cut off.

Katie remained seated as his sweaty face came into view. His breathing was ragged, his enormous chest rising and falling and his purple-gray skin flushing with a slight fuchsia undertone.

Behind him, he pulled not one, not two, but four bags of supplies through the opening. She scanned the bags, not recognizing the worn appearance of the ones she'd had with her. Had he somehow found four untouched lifeboats in the hour or so he'd been gone?

She raised her questioning gaze to him and her grudging respect must have shone through, because his mouth lifted in a smirk. He placed the packs directly in front of her like an offering, then settled nearby, his thickly corded forearms resting on his knees.

Normally, Katie would shy away from meeting the focused, unblinking stare of a handsome stranger with red eyes, but she found herself unable to look away from Maladek. She couldn't make heads or tails of this guy—grunty and domineering one minute, then dropping bones at her feet like an eager hound the next.

Too tired to solve this enigma at the moment, she dug through the packs. She divvied up the hydration tablets and nutrition bars and tossed him a portion of both. He caught them in one hand and scarfed them down without complaint.

"Make them equal," he demanded, pointing to the carefully organized piles of food and water she'd sorted.

Katie peered down at each day's rations, hers much smaller than his, and frowned at him. "You need more than I do. Look at you." She waved a hand at his impressive bulk. Her eyes caught on his exposed chest, his torn shirt hanging on by a few inches near the collar.

Throat gone dry, she popped one of the hydration tablets into her mouth. They were nowhere near as satisfying as liquid water, but they'd do the job.

Rather than arguing with her, he frowned. His gaze strayed to her headdress, which she'd put back on, and his grimace deepened.

"What's next, Maladek?" she asked, tossing him some more food and water. "How do we find my friends without leaving this cave?"

He set his rations aside. "I have a plan, little human. Not to fret." When she continued to stare at him, making her frustration clear, he explained. "The Charkathan should be the easiest to find. The more I think about it, the less I believe he's at the sea mine. We should check the Sieliji outbuildings first. Sometimes they put the prisoners they can't control with their voice to work inside. Cleaning and cooking and such. They have borders around their buildings that prevent the prisoners from leaving lest they be electrocuted."

"And if he's not there?" she urged.

Maladek flashed a dark grin that made her stomach flip. "Then I hide and hold one of the guards until they tell me where he is. But I'll need your help for that."

"My help?" Katie choked, more surprised than anything.

He tapped his finger on the shock collar around his neck and then pointed into his ear. "They've inserted stoppers into my ears to ensure I can't block my hearing or damage it. And they have this collar locked around my neck. I've tried to take out the stoppers, but they're set to shock me unconscious whenever I try. If you pulled them out after I was rendered unconscious, though…"

Katie shook her head, raising her hands in front of her. "Oh no. That sounds like an awful idea. How do you know it wouldn't just keep shocking you until you died?"

He popped a piece of the nutrition bar she'd given him into his mouth and lifted a brow at her. "It would be a waste of a good worker. Also, the technology is primitive. It shouldn't have that level of programming. There is no way for me to help you if they remain in my ears. One note from a Sieliji and I'm their instrument."

Maladek inched closer until he was sitting directly across from her with only an emergency pack separating them. Reaching forward, he pulled her wrist to him and placed the remaining half of his nutrition bar into her hand. Katie stared at it. He nudged the underside of her upturned palm, wordlessly urging her to eat.

"But once I have the stoppers out," he continued, "I can block up my ears so their song won't affect me. Then all we'll need to do is find the key for this." He tapped on his collar again, then stared at the uneaten bar in her hand. Ruby red eyes narrowing and jaw going rigid, he raised his stern gaze to her bewildered one.

Pretense and subtlety forgotten, Katie blurted, "What's the catch, Maladek? What do you want in exchange for your help?"

He raised a heavy eggplant colored brow. "I want you to eat."

"Yes, but besides that. Are you just a nice, if not incredibly odd, man? Do you really just want to help me?"

"I gave you my word. You freed me, and this is how I repay you. And…" His hands twitched where they rested on his thighs. His focus wandered over to the packs as though he were choosing his words carefully, before his gaze steadily returned to hers. "I want you to like me, Katie."

He began digging in the pack before she could respond to his utterly ridiculous answer. *He wants me to like him? Why?* She frowned at the heat curling in her belly.

He pointed to her headdress, before nudging the hand she was clutching the nutrition bar with again. "Why do you wear that?"

Katie took a small bite and forced the bland food down her throat. In truth, she didn't like wearing the headdress and when she was alone, she usually didn't. But years of wearing it day in and day out had made her feel naked when it was gone. "I always wear it in front of people. Feels weird not to," she said, with a shrug. "The Charkathan I work with don't like hair and it's part of my uniform anyway, so I'm used to it."

"*I* like your hair very much," Maladek rumbled, his eyes radiating heat as he held her gaze.

"I've noticed," Katie said slowly. A zing raced over her skin at the memory of his thick fingers in her hair. "It does get uncomfortable though…the headdress. It'd be easier if I just shaved my hair off. That's what Char Tomi keeps telling me to do."

"You will not." Though his voice was no louder than normal, his words seemed to boom in the space.

She raised a brow at him while taking another bite of food. "And do you suppose you have a say in that?"

His jaw clenched and unclenched as if he were thinking through his response carefully. "I have no say, of course." He grated out the words like each one was a physical blow.

Katie nodded. "No, you don't," she agreed. He squirmed in place, and she managed to keep her grin smothered. "You can relax. I don't plan to shave it."

The tension bunching his shoulders released a fraction, and he let out a pleased hum. In truth, Katie loved her hair. It reminded her of her mother's hair. One of the only connections she had to her family on Earth. When it was long and curled down her back, she'd examine it in the mirror and remember that she'd truly belonged somewhere once.

Most of the time, she kept it cut to her chin as it was too much to manage under her headdress when it was long. Working out all the knots when washing her hair was a job in and of itself. Even short, she'd given up trying to style it on her wash days. The headdress ruined any work she put in, anyway. Raising a hand to her scalp, she groaned.

It must have looked awful when he'd seen it. After all the excitement today, it was going to take a miracle to get it clean. Reaching into one of the bags, she drew out a small bottle of the cleansing foam she'd used to wash herself with each night. She handed another to Maladek.

"Want to wash up before we electrocute you?"

7

❧

Katie was no longer yelling at him or crying, which was a start. But she'd still not fully warmed to him yet. Not looking at him with fear in her eyes was a far cry from accepting their bond when he eventually revealed it to her.

For his part, he needed no enticing. Everything about her called to him. Every time she spoke, her voice slipped against his skin like hot water. He was fascinated with the way she examined each little thing and with the way she hummed when the silence stretched out, as if she couldn't help it or perhaps didn't realize she was doing it.

He took the bottle she offered, running his fingers over her skin more than necessary during the exchange. His already aching cock pulsed at the feel of her soft palm, and he wanted to bellow in frustration.

The pure torrent of emotion, instinct, and need that had continued to pelt him since his marks appeared was overwhelming, to say the least. He had no idea recognizing a mate would be like this, and why would he? It wasn't as if they still taught young Clecanians how to deal with the demands of the bond once it emerged.

If he'd lived three hundred years ago, he'd know exactly what to expect. He'd have strategies to combat the urges now plaguing him. But as it was, Maladek felt wholly unprepared for the delectable female sitting before him.

Her pretty blue eyes flashed to his chest again. She cleared her throat. "Um, where will you go to wash up? Where should I go?"

Maladek almost crushed the bottle in his fist. She'd done it again. He was almost certain her gaze had been appreciative when she'd peered at his body. He'd told himself it was all in his head, that the bond was playing tricks on him, but he couldn't be mistaken again, could he?

"We could bathe here if you'd like." The husky growl in his voice couldn't be helped. He only hoped she didn't get scared away. But then the strangest thing happened. Her eyes roved over his body, and she let out a slow, wistful sigh.

"I think it's best we don't." She pointed down the tunnel toward a sharp bend. "I'll be over there."

Without another word, she rose and walked away, leaving Maladek with his jaw slack. What had that expression been about?

He backed away a few paces, keeping his gaze zeroed-in on the spot where she was presumably naked. He'd already learned that humans were puzzling, but Katie was downright bewildering. Tearing out of his clothing, he quickly sprayed the concentrated foam all over his hair and body, waiting while the foam bubbled and snapped, cleaning him before slicking to the floor.

For good measure, he also used the spray to clean his clothing, but paused when he got to his shirt. He left it dirty and tossed it away. Returning to their spot in the tunnel, he spread out a few heated blankets on the ground. At first, he'd argued with himself over whether to leave the blankets behind, reasoning that she could find warmth with him if there were no blankets available. But regretfully, he thought she'd notice if all the blankets were somehow missing from each pack he brought back.

It didn't take long before Katie had finished as well and joined him. He held his breath, and a surge of pride had his spine straightening when her gaze riveted to his naked chest. Her stare left a scalding trail on his skin.

"What happened to your shirt?" she finally said, settling down across from him.

Maladek had to stifle his grin when the slightest hint of her arousal hit his nose. She *did* find him appealing. Thank the gods. "It was in shambles. Not worth cleaning." He decided to try his luck. "Besides, I've noticed you enjoy looking at my body."

A light pink blush stole over her cheeks, and she gave him a small grin. "I'm sorry. You have a very nice physique. I don't often see people as muscular as you on Betuhines. I'll stop looking." She forced her gaze to the floor.

Surprise kept his lips locked together, and the silence stretched. He hadn't expected such unfiltered honesty. Especially not since only a few hours ago she'd been ready to gouge his eyes out. Any other Clecanian female would have refused conversation unless necessary, and they certainly wouldn't be admitting attraction. "You may look your fill, Katie. I like your eyes on me."

Her blush deepened, her wide-eyed gaze lifting to meet his. She cleared her throat and rubbed the palms of her hands on her drab, freshly cleaned robe.

Why did she wear such an ugly garment? She'd said it was a uniform. "How did you come to live on Betuhines?" Maladek had assumed the humans currently on Clecania were the only ones outside of Earth, but it now struck him that there could be others floating around the galaxy.

The warm blush on her cheeks faded. "I was taken from Earth fourteen years ago. They took me by accident, I think. They ended up selling me to a slaver, and then a Charkathan found me. She took me back to Betuhines and put me to work in the palace. They told me when I made back my purchase price, I was free to go."

"How long do you have until you pay off your purchase price?" Maladek would pile every jewel he'd harvested from his mountain into a ship and dump it at the palace, if that's what it took to ensure her freedom.

She clicked her tongue and looked around the room. With a small irreverent smile, she said, "Oh, about ten years ago or so."

He scraped his plated knuckles across the ground. "They broke their word?" He failed to keep the growl out of his voice as he slid toward her. The fact that she watched his movements, but didn't object to him getting closer, was a small victory.

"No. I chose to stay."

The knowledge cooled his temper. At least he wouldn't have to murder any Endrolfen royals. "You don't want to try and return to Earth?"

She sucked in a deep breath and toyed with the frayed edge of her robe. "Return to what?" Her whispered tone was full of turmoil. "With any luck, my family will have moved on. Or at least made some peace with my disappearance. My little brother will have graduated from high school by now. If I went back, I'd just be reopening old wounds. And what would I be there, anyway? Almost half my life has been spent on Betuhines."

Her watery eyes finally lifted to meet his. The pain in their light blue depths constricted his throat. "What could I say when they asked me where I'd gone? If I told them the truth, they'd probably institutionalize me. How could I live on Earth and pretend like I hadn't spent fourteen years among aliens? I'd never be able to share any of the incredible things

I've seen or done. And even if they did believe me…what would I do? I didn't finish high school. I don't even know who the president is."

She shook her head and tugged at a stray thread. "I don't know if it's selfish or kind, but I'm not the same person I was when I was taken. I can't imagine going back now."

The tortured indecision and sadness in her voice made him wish he could curl her up tight against his chest, but it wasn't the right time. Not yet.

"Are you happy on Betuhines?" he questioned. Part of him wanted her to say no. It was selfish, but if she were unhappy, he might be able to convince her to return with him to Clecania. If she was happy though… Well, he'd just have to uproot his life and follow her.

"I'm not *unhappy*," she said, shrugging. "I feel alone sometimes." Her eyes flashed up to his, then away again. "It's weird to never be around anyone who's the same as you. The Betuhinians hate my voice. The Charkathan hate my hair. There are a couple Juboms in the kitchen who can't stand my smell. My friends in the palace are wonderful, but they're different. They don't always understand why I feel lonely. They'll talk inside their heads to each other at dinner and even after all this time forget that I can't hear them. It would just be nice to be around people who I could be myself with." She let out a light chuckle, and his insides fizzled with warmth. "People who don't have to hold back their gags every time they see my eyebrows."

She peered back up at him and her face fell, her brows drawing together. "Sorry," she said with a small shake of her head. "I don't know why I'm telling you all this."

I adore every part of you. You couldn't be more perfect if you'd been carved from my dreams. If you let me keep you, I'll show you how treasured you are every day of your life. Maladek wanted to say all this and more, but fear held him back. Did he really have enough to offer her? Was he enough? Would she want him after learning how he'd arrived on this planet?

So instead, he offered something else. "I could take you back to my planet and introduce you to the humans there."

Her eyes widened. "You'd do that? You wouldn't mind letting me come with you? I promise not to be a nuisance. And I could totally go off on my own if you start to get sick of me." Her words came out quickly, and she shifted around in her seat, her eyes round and hopeful.

Was she worried about bothering him? The idea was laughable. Merely being close to her, kicking and screaming or not, was the most gratifying experience of his life. "I would be very happy to have you with me."

The smile she bestowed on him was so brilliant, it stole his breath.

"I think we should talk about the plan, then," she began eagerly. "When do you think we should try to get into the outbuilding?"

"Depends on how long I'm unconscious for. With any luck, we'll be able to sneak in around dusk tomorrow. The building is mostly empty at that time since all the guards are either locking the prisoners away or organizing the haul from the day."

"And how will we find my other friend? Do the Sieliji ever hold their prisoners for ransom?" she asked. While she waited for him to answer, she puttered around their small space, arranging the packs neatly against the wall, and folding the heated blankets into long rectangles and layering them on top of one another until they became soft pads on which to sleep.

Irritation with himself had him balling his fists. There were three blankets in each pack. Twelve in total. Why hadn't he thought to layer them to make the hard ground more bearable? "I don't believe they do, no. They don't typically like to shine a light on themselves."

Her brows knit as she folded yet another blanket to make a soft pillow for each of them. "Why hasn't the Alliance done something about them? By the looks of it, the Sieliji have brought down thousands of poor travelers. Shouldn't they be…I don't know…reprimanded?"

"This planet isn't part of the Alliance. Other than warning travelers that this is a dangerous area to pass through, there's not much they can do besides wipe out the Sieliji. But they won't do that."

"Why not?"

"This is who the Sieliji are. They're a predatory species, and luring ships is how they hunt. You wouldn't fault any other predator for killing you if you wandered into their territory. It would be contentious for the Alliance to approve the annihilation of a whole species because of their nature, however vile it may be."

"But I'd argue that most predators don't enslave their prey," she said thoughtfully. "It's surprising that our pilots didn't know not to travel through this region."

Fury at the danger she had been put in thanks to a thoughtless crew heated his insides, but he couldn't be too angry. Their mistake had brought his mate to him, after all. "It was a stupid thing to do. Perhaps they ignored the warnings without doing their research for some reason."

"Prince Skendro *did* demand that we go home immediately, and I think the crew was rather new."

"Prince Skendro?" Maladek froze. The Endrolfen royal family was well-known throughout the galaxy. Rich, generous, and very, very powerful. Katie had explained that she worked at the palace, but he'd assumed she'd been traveling with some lower dignitary. "Is that who your other companion is?"

"Yes, I was one of the prince's attendants on the cruise. My friend, Char Tomi, was another." Katie's lips scrunched as she took in his rigid form. "Why? Does that change things? Do you think they'll ransom him?"

Maladek wanted to shout in relief at the luck he'd encountered. "This may all be much easier than we thought. If the prince is here, then all we need to do is find a way to get a message to an Alliance port. His family would do anything to get him back, and they're beyond powerful. If they found out he was being held here, they'd send reinforcements. Most wouldn't venture so close to the Sieliji planet without good cause, but for the Endrolfen Prince? All we'd have to do is wait for an army to arrive."

Katie scooted toward him, excitement shining in her crystalline eyes. She'd done the same thing in the trench, ventured too close without realizing it. Both then and now, Maladek had to rein in every instinct clamoring inside not to reach out and pull her to him. He eyed the horrible headdress she wore that covered the mounds of curling hair, and memories of her scent slammed into him. Sunshine and sweetness.

"Do you know where to find something like that?" she breathed, her lyrical voice tenderizing every stiff muscle in his body.

"I do." He dug his nails into his thighs to keep from reaching out and grabbing her. "This requires a change of plan. Once both my stoppers are out, we'll head toward the beacon and attempt to send out a message. We can look for your friends after that, while we wait for rescue."

Katie grinned, and it was as if the ever-burning fire in his mountain's communal hearth were warming his skin.

"So, how do I take those things out of your ears?"

His grin faded. This would not be pleasant.

***

"You've searched for hours now," she complained as Maladek dragged an enormous stone in front of the opening to the outside tunnel. "You said it'll take days to get there. The sooner we start, the sooner we can be on our way."

Though he'd ventured as far as he could in both directions and found no signs of danger, Maladek was still ill at ease. He stared at the stone blocking the entrance to the other tunnel. Was that a crack in the side? Maybe he should find a different barricade. She let out a huff behind him when he didn't respond. It was true he'd stalled far longer than he'd needed to.

"Have you made the hook?" he asked, looking back and forth in the tunnel once again, trying to calm his nerves. He didn't mind the inevitable pain of the electricity, but he abhorred the idea of being rendered immobile. What if she needed him? What if he was out for too long and a Sieliji found the tunnel?

What if she has a stray thought she wants to share, and I'm not awake for her to talk to? Being parted from his mate, even in sleep, sent a pang through his chest.

Katie held up the metal pins she'd fashioned into a sturdy hook. A long strip of fabric was tied to the other end. His attention drifted to the cushioned bed to her right.

It was plusher than the one she currently sat on. Had she given him extra blankets to make him more comfortable? The thought settled in his chest, squeezing on his heart.

She motioned toward the luxurious mattress and held up her hook. "I'm ready if you are." Katie grinned, exposing her small white teeth. Maladek took it as a personal victory that her smile had appeared with more frequency as the night went on. His mate was quick to happiness, and somehow her mere presence tugged his own joy out of a dark, recessed corner he'd forgotten existed.

He trailed over to her and knelt between the blankets. She let out a squeal of surprise when he wrapped his hands around her waist and transferred her to the softer of the two beds. Before she could argue, he held up a hand. "I'll not hear of you sleeping on a less comfortable surface than me." He lay down on his side and brushed his hair away from his ear.

Her lips quirked upward and though he could tell she wanted to squabble, she also seemed pleased. But soon the smile vanished, and she raised her chin, steeling her nerves. "Are you ready?"

He nodded, then stopped abruptly. "No, wait. I got you something," he said, pulling his gift from his pocket. He held it out to her, breath catching in his chest. Would she like it?

It was nowhere near as fine a specimen as he could find in his mountain. He'd sensed the treasure while on his exploration of the tunnel, and the opportunity to give her a token of his affection was too good to pass up.

She tilted her head to the side as she stared at the gleaming blue stone. He'd carved at it with a sharp rock from the tunnel wall so she could see the potential of the gem. When it was cut properly, it would sparkle.

Would she find it subpar? It pained him to think so. In his home, when a Tetran wanted to court someone, they'd leave gems they'd mined at their doors. If they were still there the next night, the gift had been rejected. Would she accept his?

"Where did you find this?" she asked, lifting it and twirling it between her fingers near the lantern light.

"I could sense a small deposit on my walk, so I dug a little." Apprehension and embarrassment rumbled through him when she continued to examine it. "There were other stones that were a finer quality perhaps," he rambled. Why hadn't he picked one of those? "But I thought the color of this one matched your eyes. I could get a different one for you if you'd like."

She eyed him with a dreamy smile. "This is the sweetest thing anyone's ever given me. Not to mention the prettiest." Her hand rested against his forearm. The muscles in his body jumped under her touch, and sparks ignited all over his skin. Though she didn't realize what it meant to him, her acceptance of his gift brought him immeasurable joy.

The light of the lantern was a mere flicker compared to the happy glow radiating from his Katie. If he ever got her back to his mountain, he'd shower her with gifts as often as he could. "All right, you may proceed," he said, suddenly impatient to get this over with so he could, in fact, get her off this planet.

She gently set the stone down on her pillow and gazed at it for a moment longer before inhaling a large breath, her expression growing serious. "All I have to do is hook this onto the tab and pull? And you're sure it won't kill you or hurt you too badly?"

"Yes, this is how the guards remove the stoppers, so it shouldn't be too difficult. But remember to only touch the string. Anything else, and you may be shocked, too."

Katie leaned forward until she was perched over his ear and gently dropped her hook. He should be paying attention to what she was doing, but the swell of her breasts hovering above his face made his mind go fuzzy. His fingers clamped around the bedding underneath him, his teeth grinding.

"I think I got it," she said, scooting away from him. With the fabric wrapped around her fist, she took a deep breath. "On the count of three." Worry pulled her mouth into a thin line.

He nodded.

"One, two—" Before she got to three, she wrenched her fist back. Shooting pain flared through his veins a moment before everything went black.

8

The rippling muscles of his back glinted in the lamplight as Maladek tore through the stone at the end of a dark tunnel. Katie held in a sigh as she watched him work, hand in her pocket, fingers twirling around the beautiful gem he'd given her. She bit her lip as he repositioned his stance and ran the backs of his fingers over a crack in the dark stone.

Heavy brows dipped in concentration, he took his time feeling the rock. He pressed his palm to its surface and let his eyes slide shut, going still and calm as if waiting for the stone to speak to him. They'd been carving their way through the cave system of this planet since he'd awoken yesterday, and she'd seen him do this often. Each time, she became more fascinated.

He turned and caught her practically salivating. She glanced away, frustration souring her mood. Even though he'd said he didn't mind her looking, she didn't want to lead him on. He was a different species, just like all the other alien crushes she'd ever had. One failed courtship after another had taught her that she just wasn't compatible with non-humans. Sexually or emotionally.

After her last fiery car wreck of a tryst wherein her male lover's semen had given her chemical burns, she'd been left disheartened and had promised herself to take it slow the next time she met someone she liked. Slow enough to research whether any part of them could injure her, at the very least.

Still, she couldn't help but daydream about Maladek. What would it be like to be with a man who was so handsome and generous and strong?

After he'd passed out, Katie had tried to get some sleep like they'd planned, but it'd been difficult for her not to admire him. She was ashamed to say she'd even run her fingers along the strong lines of his face, turning into mush when his tense jaw relaxed under her touch.

Katie still couldn't believe how quickly he'd recovered, either. It felt like she'd only been asleep for an hour when she was being gently woken. He'd demanded they remove the other stopper, which had caused a heated argument. Katie wanted to give him more time to recover, but he wanted it to be done with. In the end, she'd given in, though she agonized over him the whole time he was out, checking and re-checking his pulse.

When his eyes had creaked open and he'd caught her brushing hair off his forehead, a rumbling purr had emanated from his chest. The sound had raised goosebumps on her skin. Heat pooled in her core.

Unless she was completely misreading his signals, which she doubted since they were by no means subtle, Katie believed Maladek was attracted to her, too. Maybe when they finally left this planet and were on their way to Clecania, he'd be open to exploring this attraction more. She hoped she wasn't a temporary fascination. Her stomach roiled. Or was she just the first woman he'd come across in a while? She hadn't asked him how long he'd been here, after all. What if he had someone waiting for him back on Clecania? Or what if he lost interest once he saw some gorgeous, horned woman walk by?

"Things need to settle," Maladek called, patting the gleaming black rock like he was praising it. A smile spread over her face at the odd gesture, but she smothered it before he faced her again.

Stepping down from his elevated platform of crumbling rock, he shook out his hair and clothing. Pebbles plinked on the ground as he swept the debris away.

"I still don't understand how you can tell. Or how you know which direction to go in," she said as he stooped to retrieve a hydration tablet.

"I can sense it. I know generally where we were, and I know which direction the beacon is. My kind, Tetrans, are used to navigating underground. I can't explain it, but we all have an irrefutable sense of direction."

"And what about these tunnels?" she asked. "How did you know they were here?" He stepped closer, much closer than he needed to be for the casual conversation. Why didn't she have the urge to move away?

"Like I said, they were forcing me to mine them. It's what my kind are known for. These tunnels were made by the quallie when this area was underwater, and there are lots of valuable resources that could be harvested from them, but the Sieliji don't like risking cave-ins to do it."

Katie froze, her shoulders hiking. "The worms? These are their tunnels?"

Maladek let out a rumbling chuckle at her horror-stricken expression. He extended his hand as if wanting to touch her, but then dropped it. "Don't worry. They live in tunnels under the water and only come out at night to hunt. Their skin is too sensitive for the sun during the day. These tunnels are ancient. The quallie won't want to use them. Too dry."

"And you can just sense that?" Katie asked. She had to tilt her head to look up into his rich, ruby eyes. "How?"

He considered her question for a moment while smoothing the hair between his horns and shaking out dust. "I can *feel* it." He waved at the stone wall behind her. "I can feel where the depth of the stone is thinner, and I can perceive the empty pockets."

She must have still looked confused, because the corner of his mouth tipped up. He grabbed her wrist and turned her toward the wall of the tunnel. Katie tried to keep the fluttering in her belly quiet, as he pressed her palm against the gleaming stone.

"What can you feel here?" he asked, letting his hand loosely circle her wrist. Katie couldn't feel anything except the cold rock under her palm and her own heartbeat pounding in her ears. He slid his hand to cover the top of hers and stepped close behind. His heat seeped into her back, and she swallowed hard.

Though she knew he was waiting for her to make some kind of statement about what she could feel from the wall, she couldn't focus. His palm felt warm and smooth on top of hers, the width and length of his large hand completely engulfing her own. His fingers and knuckles had hard plates laid over the top as well, like armor or dragon scales. Curling, purple designs ran over every inch of his hand up to his wrist and undermined the deadly plating that allowed him to punch through rock as if it were paper.

The combination of his massive, towering form looming so close to her back, the softness of his skin on hers, and his warmth cocooning every inch of her made her sway.

He crouched down to her ear, whispering, "Can you feel it? Everything has a pulse. Vibrations traveling through the stone make it easy to sense what's on the other side. It's how I know the tunnel hasn't settled yet. I can feel the result of my digging echoing through the earth even now. But when I touch over here"—he wrapped his other arm around her shoulder, pointing at an area to the right—"the vibrating echo stops short. It tells me there's an empty space there."

Maladek's large chest brushed against her back, making liquid heat drip down her sex. She swallowed. Katie needed to get a hold of herself. This was no time to be mooning over a stranger.

"That's incredible." Hoping her voice wasn't as shaky as it felt, she tugged her hand out from under his and turned in his arms. Not moving an inch, his palms remained in place, his brawny arms caging her in at her shoulders. "And the plating on your hands is how you can break through without being hurt?"

He tilted his head as he stared down at her heated cheeks. His nostrils flared and a light purr rumbled in his chest. With a silent nod, he brought his hand in front of her, lifting his knuckles so she could examine the hard plates.

An internal argument waged within her for only a moment before curiosity won out. She tentatively lifted her hand and ran her fingertips over the ridged plates. They were as hard as steel.

The purr in his chest intensified as she trailed a fingertip over the bright purple marks on his thumb. A deep inhale was all she could manage when his other arm dropped to wrap around her back, tugging her closer. The heavy air crackled between them.

Her stomach dipped and sent a bolt of electricity pulsing through her sex when he squeezed her lower body to his, and she felt his hardening length press into her belly. The shock of it helped bring her back to reality, though. She pressed a hand to his chest, ignoring the firmness of the broad, naked muscle under her palm.

"I don't think this is a good idea."

He didn't move away at first, only frowned down at her.

Then his hand lifted from her waist. His fingers curled under her chin, and he tipped her head up, craning his neck forward until he met her gaze. "I can scent you want me, female."

Heat raced from her forehead to her toes. Katie knew there were many species able to smell far more than she could ever dream. Humans were practically blind, their senses were so underdeveloped. "I know, but I just don't think it's a good idea right now." She couldn't go through another awkward or potentially dangerous sexual encounter.

She tried to move away, but he backed her into the wall, brows furrowed. "So you admit you want me? Then I don't see the problem. Explain."

"It's not the right time to try and see what our compatibility is," she breathed out, shoulders slumping as frustration took hold. "I've…tried with others, and it's never worked out. Either I can't please them, or they can't please me, or I don't know enough about their customs, or we're just completely incompatible. You don't even know what I…have…you know? Why don't we just wait until we get off this planet? Then we can do some research and maybe…I mean, if you still want…" Katie slammed her mouth shut and tried to look away. She was babbling now, embarrassment making her vibrate with emotion.

She'd had some good experiences in the past, but they'd always fallen short. The tryst with the Anedde had been exceptional. The female had had suckers that she'd put to good use, but Katie hadn't had the anatomy to reciprocate.

And the Masquanith trader she met selling exotic fruit in the kitchens had been a wonderful kisser, but his kind didn't engage in penetrative sex.

Though it may seem trivial to some, her inability to be physical with another person had weighed on her heavily. It remained a stark reminder that she was alone and didn't belong. That she might never find anybody she could connect with or fall in love with. Not in the ways she craved.

Obviously, there were many ways to love and not all of them were physical, but the raging hormones of her fifteen-year-old self had never quite moved past her curiosity about sex. Of being with someone of her own species. Someone who was meant to fit with her. Maladek beamed at her, a grin spreading across his face.

He must think she was so silly. So inexperienced.

Katie tried to bob around him, embarrassment heating her face until she was sure she was beet red. He gripped her elbow to stop her from walking away, and she let out a sigh.

"We *are* compatible, Katie."

She blinked at him. He couldn't possibly know that, could he? He *had* said there were humans on his planet. "I know you look like me…kind of," she started, eyes catching on the horns sprouting from his head.

His hand snaked around her back. This time, he pulled her against his body with a rough confidence that stole her breath. His grin remained wide. "I *know* we are. A fact. Humans and Clecanians have mated on my planet."

Katie faintly recognized that her jaw had dropped. "You mean it will be pleasant? For both of us?"

Maladek stooped and brushed his mouth over the column of her neck, and she shivered. "It will be beyond pleasant. The cries I'll ring from you will echo for miles through this tunnel." Katie whimpered as both his words and his hot tongue slid over her skin.

She couldn't breathe. Her head was spinning. She already knew she liked Maladek, but now…she could truly explore him and open herself up to him. And crazier still, he seemed like he wanted her, too.

The sudden realization that a new world of possibilities lay open to her had her stomach somersaulting. This was all moving too fast. How could she even have these romantic thoughts when the prince and Char Tomi were still imprisoned, or worse…

She wrenched away from the glorious man lavishing her neck with scorching kisses, confident that if she let him continue, she wouldn't be able to stop.

Maladek let out a growl when she put space between them. Eyes gone black, it only took a second before he stalked toward her.

Katie held up her palms. "Give me a bit to get used to this, okay? Yesterday, I was pretty sure I'd be alone forever." Her words turned sour on her tongue. *Just because we're compatible doesn't mean he wants me forever.* "And if we can dig again, we should." She gestured to the area he'd been working. "Sending out a message is our first priority, right?"

Maladek's dark eyes remained trained on her, his enormous frame rigid as he listened. For a moment she thought he might be angry with her for turning him down, but then he let out a half growl, half sigh. She didn't know if a more perfect sound of frustration existed.

He crossed to her slowly, and Katie braced herself. "All right, my beautiful Katie. As soon as you sort your thoughts, you need only call, and I'll show you what could be between us." His voice was gentle, though his expression was hard. Before he turned back to work, he placed a soft kiss on her cheek.

* * *

She was one step closer to being his. Whatever power Maladek was channeling to hold himself back from his mate must surely be mighty. Her reddened cheeks had faded to a lovely, flushed pink and, beneath her ugly robe, her chest rose and fell with deep breaths.

He could tear the garment away. Run his tongue over her skin in the way that had rendered her boneless. But she'd asked him to wait, and he would. He shook his head, trying to clear his mind.

"Are you sure I can't help?" Katie asked again.

Maladek smiled and shook his head. She'd already asked to assist him many times. At first, he'd taken her offer as a slight. As if he weren't strong enough to carve a path for her. But after taking in her eager expression and restless posture, he realized that she truly just wanted to ease his burden. His little mate was thoughtful and caring.

In the short time he'd known her, she'd done nothing but put others first. As they'd traveled, she'd regaled him with the story of her crash. Even in the face of such terror, she'd made sure to save as many as she could. And she was *his* mate. Pride swelled in his chest, then uncertainty deflated it.

For the rest of his days, he would never want anyone else, but she might never feel the same. Maladek felt like he'd burst if he had to keep the significance of his marks to himself for much longer. She'd agreed to come with him to Clecania. He had time. Once he gentled her toward the idea of mating and everything that went along with it, he'd explain that he recognized her. He peered over his shoulder and nearly groaned. She was eyeing his back again, her small lower lip pulled between her teeth.

Turning back toward the hard stone, he curled his fist. Fragments of rock the size of boulders fell with booming thuds as he took out his frustration on the tunnel wall.

9

"Do you think the Sieliji will come out to patrol these tunnels once they realize you've escaped?" Katie asked as she climbed over a mini rockslide blocking their path. They'd been walking for a few hours now and the cave system had gradually changed, the smooth glassy walls becoming matte black and porous. The perfectly round shape of the tunnel had morphed too. She could still see the path of whatever ancient quallie had burrowed through here, but the walls were no longer smooth and unbroken. Instead, long crevices and alcoves pocked every inch of the stone.

"No," he answered from behind her.

The warmth and strength of his hands made her movements slow as he gripped her waist to steady her. Katie had the uncharacteristic urge to feign clumsiness and slip.

Would he sweep her up into his arms if she did? Regretfully, he released his hold once she'd cleared the loose rock and walked beside her instead.

"They hibernate during the night," he explained. "That's why they lock themselves up. They go into a sort of stasis and are unable to defend against an attack. They wouldn't risk exploring the caves this far since they'd be forced to spend the night unprotected."

The warm, spicy scent of his heated skin made her want to bury her face in his chest. She inhaled through her mouth. "How do you know so much about them, anyway?"

"I made sure to learn all I could." His eyes shifted to her for a moment before he glanced away. "I came here willingly."

Katie's steps faltered, and she couldn't help but stare. "What? Why?" A pinched look crossed his face in the dim, swinging light of the lantern. Whatever his answer might be, it wasn't something he wanted to talk about. "It's all right. You don't have to tell me."

Maladek let out a breath. "No. I want you to know all of me. The good and bad."

A shiver skittered down her spine at his words. The idea was so innocuous yet sounded so intimate when uttered in his deep, gravelly voice. As if he didn't merely *want* her to know all his secrets, but *craved* it.

"I was in a bad way with an illegal trader." He dug in the pack as he talked and handed her a nutrition bar. Katie took it, torn between staying silent for his story and thanking him for his thoughtfulness.

No one ever took care of her like this anymore. Since she'd been abducted, taking care of others had become her whole life. She found she liked him tending to her needs far more than she should. Getting used to this kind of treatment was a dangerous thing.

"My father worked as a master carver in our mountain, and he took on a young apprentice who showed a fair bit of skill. The boy practically grew up in my house and became something of a little brother to me. But he was always so headstrong. Never satisfied with his life there. He wanted to venture out and explore the universe, so when he came of age, he did.

"Unfortunately, the universe proved to be more than he'd bargained for. He'd gotten in with this female and her illegal operations. She'd promised him travel and excitement in exchange for his loyalty. On one of the runs he made for her, he saw an innocent killed and realized how out of his depth he was. He tried to beg his way out of his contract, but she refused, so he ran back home. The female wouldn't let it lie. I went to her, and in exchange for my help with a particularly important run, she agreed to forgive his debt to her."

Maladek's gaze was shuttered, a deep line between his brows. Katie wanted to take hold of his hand, give him support. She eyed his hand and arm swinging so close to hers. If she just stepped over a little, their skin would brush. "What did she have you do?"

"I was to infiltrate a crew and ensure the captain of the ship followed her instructions. It seemed simple enough, so I agreed. At one time, this captain had been her right-hand man and from what I gathered, her lover, but she'd grown distrustful of him and wanted to make sure his loyalty remained intact." He let out a groan. "Unfortunately, her instincts were right and his priorities *had* shifted. She learned of it and made a deal with the Sieliji. She commanded I take over the ship and land it on this planet so she could retrieve her package and leave the crew behind as payment to the Sieliji for allowing her to use their world as a secure exchange location for her goods."

Katie raised a hand to her mouth. "She left a whole crew behind just so she could get her order? What was the shipment? What could have been so important?"

He hurled a small stone down the hallway with a growl. It sailed out of sight into the blackness and made the faintest ping when it landed. "To this day, I don't know." His head dipped, and he shook it, shame tightening the lines bracketing his mouth. "We were to find out when we picked it up. She'd given us leave to ensure the contents were undamaged, but I came to my senses before that. Even the threats against my friend Biroun weren't enough to justify leaving all those people to die. So, I helped cause a distraction, then I stayed behind and fought off the Sieliji so the crew could flee."

Katie reached out, no longer able to hold back, and twined her fingers with his. "You did the right thing."

Maladek stopped in his tracks and stared down at their joined hands, brows lifted. *Oh no. I shouldn't have grabbed him.* She tried to pull away, but he tightened his hold and glanced up at her, a silent request for her to remain in place. Fluttering started up in her belly.

He began walking again, absently caressing her thumb with his own. After a few moments of silence, he muttered, "It wasn't the right thing. I did the wrong thing, then tried to make up for it. There's a difference."

When Katie let out a light chuckle, he furrowed his brows at her. "That's all anyone can do. No one makes the right decision every time. Everyone makes mistakes. You shouldn't feel bad for being human…or…I mean…being imperfect."

His ruby eyes glinted in the lantern light as he looked ahead, silently considering her words. Eventually, his chin lifted, his spine straightening. She couldn't be sure, but Katie believed her words had resonated, and he'd finally left behind some of the guilt that had been weighing him down.

As they continued walking, Katie told Maladek all about her childhood on Earth and her new life on Betuhines. It was odd to try and recall details about Earth. Like a dream you couldn't quite remember. Some information like her address and her old phone number were locked in a vault, but other things were hazy. She remembered she'd had band posters on her bedroom wall, but for the life of her, she couldn't remember which bands. Her favorite restaurant served the best pierogi in North Dakota, but she couldn't remember the name of the restaurant or what street it was on.

Maladek had listened intently as she reminisced about her outgoing mother's love of pro wrestling and her soft-spoken father's devotion to their family and his love of insects, which he'd passed onto her little brother Bradley. Then Katie had faltered. She'd tried to picture their faces in her mind and…couldn't.

Somehow realizing the pit in her belly and clog in her throat were preventing her from speaking, Maladek squeezed her hand, still clasped in his, and stepped infinitesimally closer. His deep, gravelly voice soothed her as he told her about the mountain range he and his people lived in back on Clecania. Visions of intricately carved stone caverns and glittering gem-inlaid tapestries filled her mind, wiping out the cold sadness from a moment ago. She watched him closely as he described the sprawling home he'd spent years excavating and just about melted at the warm smile lighting his face.

Somehow, she felt so connected to Maladek and though she couldn't understand why, she found herself more interested in seeing the place he spoke about with such nostalgia than she did about meeting the other humans. Would he agree to take her if she asked? Katie wasn't sure what Maladek wanted from her other than the obvious, but the fact that he hadn't released her hand since she'd reached out for him gave her hope that his feelings went beyond the physical.

The path degraded more and more as they continued walking, making conversation difficult. No longer were only the walls marked with large holes and brittle rock, but the floor as well. Katie just managed to sidle past a deep hole in the ground that took up over three-fourths of their walkway when an ominous rumble shook the walls. Maladek's grip on her tightened as they both froze, listening to the small pings of stones hitting the ground.

He reached out and placed his hand on the wall. Eyes moving across the ceiling as if he could see through it, he said, "Quallie. It must be night because they're roaming. This tunnel shouldn't collapse, but I think we should find a place to rest for the night until morning."

Katie agreed easily. Her feet and leg muscles already ached from walking for so many hours. They continued on a little longer. Every rumble of the fragile rock made the thick muscles of Maladek's back tense more and more until he was fully flexing, his body the picture of perfect musculature. She hated that he was so on edge, but she didn't hate the view.

When his drawn expression didn't fade after they'd found a small, sturdy-looking alcove to crowd into for the night, Katie spoke. "If you're sure it won't cave in, why do you look so nervous?"

He spread their blankets out on the ground, and she was disappointed to see he'd made two pads rather than one large one. She hadn't asked him to share a bed with her, but the space was cramped enough that a small piece of her hoped he'd take the initiative. "I've checked the walls. They're sturdy. But the quallie are heavy. If enough settle in the wrong spot…" His strong jaw tightened, and he tilted his head upward. "I'll stay up tonight."

His drawn expression as he glared up at the comparatively intact stone surface of their alcove made her heart squeeze. "Will you have a fit if I leave to wash up?" she asked, holding up a bottle of concentrated cleanser.

His hand remained planted on the wall. He frowned at the small bottle. "Make it quick. And don't go far," he called after her as she rushed away.

"I'll stay right outside." She planted herself just out of sight of the entrance to their makeshift bedroom and had removed one pin from her headdress when heavy footsteps made her turn.

Maladek stood on the other side of the opening, back turned to her. From over his shoulder, he said, "I need to bathe too, and I don't like you being out alone. I'll know if the tunnel becomes unstable more quickly than you will."

Katie's fingers remained frozen to her headdress. She should demand he move further away or at least make him promise he wouldn't peek at her, but she didn't. Would he look if she didn't tell him not to? She kept her gaze trained on him for a moment longer, wondering what it'd be like to boldly strip down and bathe in front of this man. But when he started toying with the front of his pants, she flushed, and turned away.

There was a constant prickling along the skin at her back as she undressed and sprayed the foam over her body. It was like the knowledge that they were both naked and only a few feet apart tinged the air with electricity. She worked her fingers into her hair more vigorously than she previously had. Her curls would still look like a mess without any way to style or deep condition them, frizzy and puffy and kinked in the wrong places, but she didn't want to sleep in her headdress again. Nonstop use had given her a headache, and the weight of the fabric caused an ache to pulse down her neck. That's how she justified scrubbing her scalp and tearing her fingers through her curls, anyway. It definitely wasn't an excuse to keep her headdress off because some particularly incredible alien man liked her hair.

She waited as the foam cleaned the dirt from the rest of her body, ears straining past the crackle and fizz, listening for movement from behind her. When the slippery sound of skin sliding against skin sent a rush of heat through her belly, she distracted herself by spraying her clothing with foam, concentrating on the bottom hem, which was the dirtiest. Her thin underdress was clean before anything else, so she put that on and waited for the foam to finish working its magic on her robe and headdress.

Rumbling shook the walls all around her and, on instinct, she glanced over to Maladek. He was far closer than he'd been before. And he was watching her. Ruby red irises now suffused with black as dark as the stone walls, he stared.

The tunnel vibrated harder, and small chunks of rock plunked onto the ground all around her.

"We'll come back for your clothes when the quallie have moved on," he said in a voice gone hoarse. His eyes flared and his hands shot out to haul her against his chest a moment before a baseball-sized piece of rock fell where she'd been standing.

Katie's skin hummed with awareness. Her breaths came in quick pants. Not because a rock had almost split her skull open, but because she was flush against his bare chest. The only thing separating them, her thin underdress. Before, through the thick, rough fabric of her robe, he'd felt good. But now? Pure heaven. His body was warm and firm. Thick layers of muscle pressed pleasantly into the soft flesh of her breasts.

She wanted to bask in his hold. Run her hands up his strong shoulders and feel them bunch under her palms. But he swept her away and deposited her in the alcove before taking a few hasty steps back. His one long horn scraped against the sloped ceiling as his back hit the wall, but he didn't even wince. His dark stare remained glued to her, his fists clenching and unclenching, until he abruptly turned his back and faced the wall.

Katie grinned. It was as if he'd put himself in a timeout. Unsure what else to do, she knelt on her pad and waited. He shook his head, trying to dislodge some errant thought apparently, then ran his hands in between his horns, smoothing his dark purple hair.

Deciding that some privacy might be respectful, she dug in one of the packs and set out some food and water on his pad. Eyes darting to make sure he was still preoccupied with the wall, Katie covertly tugged his pad a few inches closer to hers.

She was about to change her mind and slide the pad away again when Maladek faced her. The red of his eyes was once again visible.

Not quite avoiding her gaze, but not catching her eye either, he relaxed onto his pad and reclined against the stone wall. His palm flattened on the ground next to him, and her heart warmed. Always on alert. Always keeping them safe.

"What happened to your horn?" she asked, examining the smooth surface of his right horn again. His attention had been far off, his gaze continuing to creep toward her before shooting away. But at her question, his features hardened, brows lowering ominously and shadowing his eyes. His fingers brushed over the smooth surface of his horn. "The Sieliji like to…take pieces when I'm entranced."

Katie's jaw froze in the middle of chewing a dry nutrition bar. "They what? Why? Were they just trying to hurt you? Oh my God, does it hurt?" Katie cried, dropping the bar on the pad and scooting toward him. She'd been so oblivious. Had he been in pain this whole time? Her fingers flinched. She wanted to reach out and stroke his horn, soothe an old injury, but she kept her fists at her sides. What if it still hurt him?

A small smile curled his full lips as he studied her expression. "Are you concerned for me, beautiful Katie? No, it doesn't hurt. My horn will grow back in time. It's more insulting than anything else. Some like to powder it and put it in their drinks as an aphrodisiac."

Katie curled her lip in disgust. "What wretched little things. It's one thing to have you do labor, but it's another thing to take part of you and…consume it. Why would they even think to do that?"

With a low chuckle, Maladek settled his weight on his right arm and leaned forward, brushing his fingers over her hair by her temple. "They probably thought to do it because my horn *is* an aphrodisiac."

Katie didn't know what to say to that. Surprise and the pleasurable tingling sensation of someone playing with her hair kept her still and wide-eyed.

"It's insulting because we cut our horns with our mate. It's a Tetran ritual. Couples use the powder in a special drink called vishou. We share it before we have sex. To see a male Tetran walking around with cut horns will earn him respect and envy. But if his horns were damaged in a fight or broken or, in my case, stolen, it's a vicious blow to our pride. The longer and stronger the horns, the more virile a male is thought to be."

A question, a completely inappropriate one, bubbled up in Katie's throat. *How big are your horns compared to other men?* She just managed to hold her tongue, and instead asked, "Have yours ever been broken before?"

A second after she'd asked, she wondered if the question was rude, but Maladek nodded thoughtfully, his gaze still leisurely roaming over her uncovered hair. "Yes, quite often when I was younger. Our people enjoy a good brawl. You can always tell which young males need more time to mature because their horns will be broken and uneven. Once a male can keep them protected and win in fights, he's thought of as strong enough to take a wife." Maladek's gaze met hers. "Mine have not been broken for decades now, Katie."

She shivered at the implication, though she needed no proof that Maladek was all strong, capable man.

He let out a sigh. "Not until recently, that is. Injuring your horns in a fight is one thing. It's embarrassing but fair, and only strengthens you in the long run. But to *take* something sacred that should be reserved for my mate is beyond dishonorable." His eyes roved down her body as he spoke, lingering on the straps of her dress tied in a loose knot at her nape.

The tunnel shuddered, and Maladek snatched her mat, yanking it toward him until she sat cross-legged in between his wide, bent knees. Echoes of falling rock boomed through the space, but Katie barely flinched, her attention completely consumed with Maladek. It was so strange that in a place like this, after surviving what she'd survived, she was completely unfazed by the stone crumbling around her. He would keep her safe. She had no doubts.

Maladek looked up, and he smoothed his palm to the wall behind him with closed eyes.

Katie licked her lips. "What does it feel like?" she breathed.

"I believe it's settling. The—"

"No," she interrupted. Her cheeks heated with her blush, but she couldn't contain her curiosity. "Drinking vishou."

His eyes flashed open and leveled on her, one brow raised.

"How does it make you feel?" She leaned forward as she spoke, and fire flickered in Maladek's red eyes. Inky blackness crept in from the corners, consuming the white.

"Would you like to try some, little female? Would you like to drink me in?" The deep purr of his voice dripped over her like warm honey and pooled in her low belly.

There was no sense in denying it. "Yes," she breathed. "What would happen?"

Holding her wide gaze, he slid his hands over her hips, then gripped her ass. Using his grip, he dragged her forward until her knees hit his inner thighs. "I'd lead you to our vishlouti room and offer you a honed crystal cup to drink from." He wrapped his palms around her crossed legs and gently, but firmly, pried them apart, then draped one leg over each of his massive thighs. Spice and something dark and earthy hit her nose as he leaned forward. His imposing frame still loomed above her, even though they were both seated.

Katie's breath hitched when he exhaled against her ear. "First, you'll start to feel sensitive, every touch stronger than before." Goosebumps broke out over her skin as he skimmed his sharp, plated knuckles over her bare upper thighs.

At this angle, her legs were spread apart, her underdress hiked up. She could already feel hot liquid arousal coating her entrance, readying her body for him. And Maladek knew exactly how he was affecting her. He'd be able to scent it. Her nipples hardened and her knees twitched when the plates of his fingers brushed against her inner thighs.

"Then you start to feel warm. Hot. Like there's a fire inside you. The heat makes you melt and thirst takes hold. You become starved for something to quench you." Katie's heartbeat fluttered inside her chest. Already, fire burned through her. His words alone causing the sensation.

He ran his fingers up her rib cage, tracing the swell of her breasts and following the straps of her dress. The sensation of the knot at her neck pulling free was buried under the sharp nip he gave to her earlobe. Katie let out a whimper, then a moan when he soothed the area with his tongue.

Her pussy throbbed, wetness seeping out from her soaked underwear to coat her thighs. She wriggled her hips, trying to inch closer to him. He let out a growl at her movements and flung his massive forearm around her back. In one smooth movement, he pulled her onto his lap so she was straddling him fully. Her hands looped around his neck, and her eyes all but rolled back at the feel of his thick, rock-hard shaft pressing along the seam of her sex.

"Would you like to know what happens next, my Katie?" he growled, kissing the underside of her jaw with slow swipes of his hot tongue. She gasped and nodded in answer, head falling back to give him better access. "I'd fuck your burning cunt until you were reduced to a mere smoldering ember. Then I'd pour vishou down your throat and fuck you again. I'd scrape my horns smooth to keep you satisfied, love." He rolled his hips against her, and a bolt of pleasure so violent it verged on pain made her jerk and moan in his hold.

Katie knew his words were only meant to turn her on, but she couldn't help but get lost in the fantasy. What if he did pick her to be his mate? What if he cut his horns for her and strutted around proudly, showing the blunted ends off as if showing her off? With low, strangled groans, he rocked his cock against the wet fabric of her panties over and over until she was bleary-eyed and panting.

Pulling her head back, she met his ravenous gaze. The dark ferocity in his wild expression tightened the knot in her low belly. Did his kind kiss? Many species didn't.

Needing to feel as connected to him as possible, she dipped her head and pressed her lips to his. When he didn't move, her heart squeezed with disappointment.

She'd pulled her lips a millimeter away when he buried his thick fingers in the hair at her scalp and held her firm. "Show me, love," he groaned.

Normally, she'd be shy about something like that. It wasn't as if she'd had much experience, but with Maladek…she was eager. Not because she didn't fear embarrassing herself, but because for some reason she knew he'd want her regardless.

The slight jerkiness of his palm clutching her ass and the stony, determined set of his jaw told her he craved this just as much as she did—and nothing she could do would change it. The knowledge made her feel heady and powerful.

She pressed her lips to his again, and for the first time in her life, stopped being self-conscious. Curiosity about how he might taste pulled at her, so she swiped her tongue across his full lower lip and was rewarded with a deep, rumbling groan. Soon he was taking control, sliding his tongue against hers and deepening the kiss until she was scalded from the inside. His intoxicating scent engulfed her and filled the dark room. The pinch of pain from his grip on her ass forced her hips to buck and grind against him.

Goosebumps followed the trail of his fingers as they slithered down from her hair to pull her dress down to her waist, exposing her breasts. He toyed with her nipples, running his thumb over the sensitive peaks until each swipe sent a pulse straight to her core. Katie tried to scoot her ass away from his cock, but he tightened his hold on her and growled, giving a quick pinch to her nipple in warning.

She tore her mouth away and kissed the strong line of his jaw, wishing she could remove his collar and kiss his neck as well. "Let me," she breathed into his ear.

A deep moan rolled out of him when she reached between them to fumble with the clasps of his pants. He let her shuffle back, realizing what she wanted. He reclined against the rock wall, both large palms now kneading her breasts.

Her fingers slowed as she caught sight of the strong, flexing muscles of his stomach and chest. Vicious scars crisscrossed all over his smooth purple skin, flushed with a deep fuchsia. Finally, she undid his pants, and he sprung free. His cock was as devastating as the rest of him—long and swollen and already pulsing under her rapt stare. The idea of him filling her with that made a strangled whimper rise in her throat.

"You'll be my undoing if you keep staring like that," Maladek rumbled through heavy breaths. Katie tried to balance herself with a squeak as he suddenly sat up. Sliding both hands under her dress and along the curve of her back, he lifted the fabric and tugged it off her raised arms.

Her underwear was still in place, but after one loud rip, they were gone too.

Maladek wrapped his immense palms over her hips, his thumbs pressing into the soft curve of her belly. He leaned back and ran his dark gaze over every exposed inch of her, ending at her dripping sex. His thighs parted, stretching her legs wide and giving him an utterly vulgar view. A loud rumbling purr erupted from his chest and echoed through their small alcove.

"Ask me to fuck you now, Katie," he grated, his black eyes lifting to hers.

Her heart stuttered, breath catching in her throat. "Please fuck me, Maladek," she panted, struggling to break his hold and plaster herself to his wide, inviting chest.

He guided her forward with his grip on her hips until she was on her knees above him, her entrance brushing the head of his cock. As he lowered her, his broad tip slid between her lips and stretched her wide. The strong purr reverberating from his chest buzzed through his whole body, including his cock. If he hadn't been holding her firmly in place, Katie would have jumped away from the intensity of it. He let her get used to the vibration and his size for a moment longer before forcing her down a few more inches.

Her body trembled as the vibration from his shaft exploded through her. Liquid heat gushed through her core, slicking her entrance and easing his way until she felt no more pain, just a hollow ache. By the time he was halfway seated inside her, she was a sloppy, whimpering mess on the verge of coming harder than she ever had before. He let out a string of curses as she rocked her hips against his hold, desperate to feel all of him.

With a snarled "Mine," he slammed her down his length until he was buried, impaling her to the hilt. It was her undoing. The orgasm that had been building to a fever pitch crested and broke over her with a bone-jarring intensity. Her scream turned into a moan, body tensing and lungs closing up as her toes curled and her eyes rolled back.

Heavenly waves of sizzling pleasure wracked her body and, somewhere in the midst of it all, she'd reached up to grip his horns. As she went boneless in his arms and he began to rock inside her once more, her fingers tightened around his horns.

Mine.

10

∾

Maladek struggled to keep his touch from hurting her, but staying in control was taking all the willpower he could muster. His mate was in his arms, moaning and writhing as he slipped in and out of her hot, tight cunt. He'd hoped placing her on top would keep her in control and keep him from rutting her like a beast, but he couldn't seem to let go of the commanding grip he had on her hips.

The sweet, bright scent of her orgasm poured into his lungs and made him drunk with need. Her thighs had almost stopped quivering against his hips, but his ears ached to hear her scream while her core convulsed around him once more before he was done. Despite himself, he found his thrusts growing rougher. Each time his skin slapped against hers, a clipped, growling groan escaped his chest.

Head dipping, he licked and sucked at her rosy nipples, hissing as the pleasurable pain from her grip on his horns intensified and sent sparks racing over his scalp. Her mewls and moans had his mind blurring and his shaft throbbing for release.

He wrapped his arms around her, one at her waist and one at her shoulder, and pressed her flush to his chest, her neck in line with his mouth. Then he clambered to his knees. Purr quaking out of his chest when she hugged his head, he began to ram into her. His hold on her remained tight as he fucked her, guiding her body where he needed.

High-pitched gasps of pleasure echoed off the walls, spurring him on. Whatever doubts lingered that he'd be too much for his small female to handle dissolved. He smelled no fear or pain. Only the hot liquid coating her insides and easing his thrusts. She was a match for him in every way. His balls slapped against her ass as his rough thrusts quickened.

Her body was strung tight, her breaths coming in short, quick pants. Her dull nails dug into the hair at his nape and her cheek rested on his forehead between his horns. The image of her clutching him like that with such trust and abandon had his purr thundering through him.

"Yes," she cried, nails digging in deeper.

His answering growl leaked out of him. His low belly pulled tight, and his cock swelled to a painful degree. Her body shuddered then, her sex convulsing as she cried out against his hair. Somehow, he managed to slow his thrusts, letting her take her pleasure once more before he did.

He tangled one hand in her hair and pulled her head back so he could look up at her. "I'm going to come inside you, Katie."

Her languid gaze flickered with hunger, and she nodded. Taking his face between her palms, she kissed him again. Heat flared through him at the feel of her small tongue licking his lower lip. He pounded into her with renewed ferocity. He'd never imagined kissing her mouth like this would drug him as it did. But now that he'd discovered the human practice, the idea of taking her mouth while spilling into her greedy cunt was something he craved more than anything else in memory.

He moaned against her mouth as his orgasm surged, then tore away and roared at the ceiling as his cock pulsed inside her, bathing her sex.

An ominous crack echoed over their panting, and Maladek swore. Still buried in his mate, he wrapped a hand around the base of her skull and flattened her to the ground, just as a portion of the cave outside crumbled.

He felt the ground while using his width to shield her and waited until the worst of the vibrations stopped.

He'd been so stupid, shouting like that in such a delicate place, but luckily he'd picked their resting spot well. It remained strong and intact around them. He gritted his teeth with a wince. She'd be angry, though. He hadn't been keeping a good enough watch, too distracted by her lush body. He lifted his head, fully expecting to find her glaring, only to be surprised when a very different emotion peered back at him. He also felt the small squirming of her hips, which he hadn't noticed a moment before.

She wasn't through with him.

A wide grin split his face and his chest expanded. Goddess, was his mate sexy. Her little yellow brows knit as she continued to rock her hips underneath him. He'd learned that human females had pleasure centers on the outside of their bodies rather than deep inside like Clecanian females, but what that meant had been lost on him until today. She was sensitive… And accessing the spot that made her moan was far too easy for him not to take advantage.

He rocked his hips into her with a slow thrust and felt her shiver. "Again, my Katie? Aren't you worried about the cave-in that just happened?"

She let out a breathless chuckle that morphed into a moan when he languorously slid in and out of her, his come and hers making her core slippery and hot. Maladek relaxed onto his elbows, bracketing them on either side of her head. He hadn't been able to see her face when her orgasm hit her before, but now he could savor the sight.

"I trust you. You won't let anything hurt me."

Maladek's grin faltered. His heart pinched at her unerring confidence in him. He slid his hands to her face and ran his thumbs over her cheeks, then her temples, warmth blooming in his chest.

"No. I won't. Never." Her gaze focused on his and her brows drew together.

Katie reached up and pulled his mouth down to hers, but this time, their kiss was slow and quiet. Maladek basked in the intimate moment, hope settling itself firmly in his soul. As the soft cries of her orgasm filled his ears, he felt sure she would accept the bond.

* * *

As soon as the wailing of the quallie had calmed and Maladek was sure the sun had risen, he gently roused Katie. He hadn't wanted to. Her serene sleeping form, draped over him, had left him floating in a daze all night. Her soft, fluffy hair tickled his arm as she twitched in her sleep, and when he ran his hand over her curls to calm her, she relaxed. He'd been afraid he would wake her when his purr started in his chest, happiness bringing it to the surface more often than ever before. But the gentle vibration had seemed to only lull her further.

Still, they needed to move. If last night had taught him anything, it was that he wanted their lives to start without any secrets between them, and for that to happen, he needed to get to the beacon and contact help.

She raised her arms over her head, stretching as he dug her robe and headdress out from under the fallen rock. Eyes widening and head swiveling around, Katie examined the large cave-in that had blocked part of the tunnel a few feet away. With a coy, surprised smile, she glanced at him. "Did you do that?"

Chuckling, he brought her robe to her, brushing off the dust that had settled in the fabric. With a crooked finger, he lifted her chin and bent his face to hers. "Darling, *you* did that." A light blush colored her cheeks, and he gave her a soft kiss.

"You'll have to be more careful next time," she murmured, donning her robe.

Pride and satisfaction surged through him at that. "Don't tempt me. The beacon should only be a short walk away now, but I'll keep you here for another day if you let me."

She gave him a flirtatious smile and reached for his hand. "Come on." With a sigh, she tugged him forward.

They didn't have to walk far before Maladek sensed thunderous activity in the distance. They were near the city, which meant they were near the beacon. Depositing her in a strong alcove, he surveyed the area and strategized the best way to dig upward and break through the surface. Katie once again offered to help, but he just frowned at her. Her delicate skin would be torn to shreds in a moment. Even hauling the sharp, porous rock would rub her palms raw after only a few loads. He liked that his mate was unafraid of hard work, but he wasn't about to let her exert herself. He had other ideas about how she might use her energy, and they involved making a very different part of her sore.

After a few hours of work, he tapped his knuckles against the ceiling and sensed only a thin layer of hard stone before dense sand. Deep breaths evening out as he worked through his next steps, he turned to peer at her. Maladek found her happily munching on a nutrition bar while watching him with covetous eyes. She grinned when he caught her staring, a playful, sexy grin that had his insides heating. "Enjoying yourself?" he asked.

Never one for subtlety, she nodded. "Very much. I like it when you get all heated. Your skin gets a little magenta. I've never met anyone as strong as you."

Maladek preened. All males on Clecania wanted to impress their partners. Not only was it part of their DNA, the male's natural instinct to show off, but it was also necessary to impress now that males outnumbered females twenty to one. If you couldn't set yourself apart, couldn't be the best, the strongest, the most handsome, the most talented, you were lost in a sea of suitors. Even with a broken horn and nothing to offer, Katie saw him. Appreciated his gifts and graced him with her lovely body.

A dark thought dimmed his joy. He turned back to his work before she could see, but a slithering voice continued to whisper to him. What if he got lost among the hordes of males once more? What if when he took her back to Clecania, she found she preferred someone else? She was his mate and every inch of him ached to satisfy her and keep her with him until death took them both, but humans didn't feel the bond the way Clecanians did. What would he do if she tired of him?

Letting his frustration power his movements, he punched through the thin rock of the ceiling and ducked as a shower of packed sand came raining down over him. He shook his hair out and wiped off his face, then piled some stones beneath him so he could peek through the small hole he'd made. Tentatively, he lifted his head into the bright world above.

He'd been close in his estimation of the distance. To the left, he could see the towering haphazardly built city the Sieliji lived in, and to his right, somewhat closer, two outbuildings, one which housed their only means of communication with the outside universe. His old boss, Klinara, had made sure to give coordinates to the beacon. It's how the Sieliji broadcast their deadly lure into space around their planet. Ships would access the message, thinking it to be a distress call.

Maladek squinted into the sky. The sun wouldn't set for a few hours, and until then, it was too dangerous to venture out. The Sieliji would be fully awake and manning the beacon. Their only chance was to wait until the fish-people were entering hibernation before striking.

Maladek ducked back inside and found Katie standing close behind. "Are we where we should be?" she asked.

"Close enough. Just a few more hours, and we can make a run for the beacon."

The grim argument raging in his chest must have shown on his face, because Katie asked, "What's wrong?"

"I'd rather you not come with me, but I really can't see a way around it. I've wondered whether the message will carry the same weight if I deliver it, but I don't believe it will. It has to be you. The palace will recognize your voice…I hope. Especially if you describe who you are. They'll be more likely to believe you and come quickly than they would me."

"That's true." She stepped up to him and swept sand off his forearm. "I wouldn't feel too conflicted, though. I would have pushed for you to take me with you either way. You don't really have a choice in the matter."

Maladek gave a low chuckle, and stepped down from the pile of rocks, closing the distance between them. "Is that so?"

She nodded. "I'm afraid you're stuck with me."

Maladek's chest constricted. All he wanted in the universe was to be stuck with her.

11

Though she was still tender from the night before, Katie took full advantage of the downtime they had, crawling atop Maladek and melting into his fevered kisses. She would have been happy for a repeat of the night before, but Maladek seemed determined to learn. As if he had something to prove. He stripped her bare and laid her on the pad before him, then spread her legs and examined her with such intensity that her cheeks flamed.

He made her explain where her clit was, and after some convincing, he forced her to touch herself. To show him what she liked. His rumbling purr of pleasure and his focused, unblinking gaze soothed her mortification. Before long, her knees had fallen wide, and she was stroking herself with abandon.

When she drew close to coming, he growled and flung her hand away. Any argument died in her throat when his warm mouth descended on her and the vibration from his purr buzzed through his tongue.

He was insatiable, lapping and delving into her until she saw stars dancing across the onyx ceiling. She never knew it could be like this. He'd been right. They were more than compatible. They fit. Were attuned to each other in a way she'd never thought possible.

Maladek was observant and learned what she liked almost more quickly than she could discern it. There was no awkward fumbling. No embarrassing explanations. Even when he asked her to clarify the differences in her anatomy, it was done with such lust-filled urgency that it turned her on rather than making her feel strange. He asked because he wanted to give her as much pleasure as possible, not because he was deciding whether her human body was worth the trouble.

When his thick tongue wrung the orgasm from her body, Katie tried to return the favor. She pushed on his shoulders, but he remained heavy and unmovable, his head collapsed on her belly. "It's too soon," he said, giving her sex another loving swipe with his tongue. She understood what he meant.

She *was* tender. But what she had in mind wouldn't worsen that condition.

Gripping his horns and tilting his head so he gazed up at her with a confident smirk of masculine satisfaction, she explained that she wanted to use her mouth on him. She had to hold in a giggle as his self-assured expression morphed, brows rising and eyes flashing black in an instant.

After a few silent moments wherein a war waged over his face, he turned her down. "No, I'm dirty. Covered in sand. And if you ever grace me with that luxury, I want to enjoy it fully. In my home."

The shaft of bright light illuminating the tunnel from the hole he'd punched in the ceiling dimmed and became the pale orange of a setting sun. With a groan, Maladek rose, giving each one of her breasts a caress before kissing her mouth and getting back to work, widening the hole in the ceiling so they could climb through.

She wondered whether he'd really take her back with him to his home, or if he'd only said it as a hypothetical—albeit lovely—scenario. The urge to push for clarification was like a living thing in her. But she didn't want to ruin whatever had bloomed between them. What if she came on too strong? What if he didn't want her to stay with him? He'd alluded to the fact that he wanted her around, but she couldn't rely too heavily on those words spoken during moments of physical intimacy. They could just be words.

Katie realized something about herself then. She was proud of her life. She'd worked for everything she had, meager as it might be, and the thought of imposing on someone made her bristle. If he wanted her to stay with him, he'd need to ask directly. She refused to take advantage of his kind nature and force herself into his life.

The hole in the ceiling expanded until it was large enough to accommodate his bulky shoulders. He gestured for her with his hand and whispered, "We'll leave the packs here and come back after we send out the message. Depending on how long this takes, we might need to run back to avoid early rising quallie, and I don't want our provisions weighing us down."

She clambered up the rickety stone pile toward him and tried to settle her raging emotions. *Focus on the task ahead.*

Maladek leapt through the hole, and after a few moments, his arm appeared, fingers outstretched. He gripped her forearm when she offered it. With surprisingly little effort, he lifted her through the roof and placed her next to him on the sand. Not a second passed before she was shielding her eyes. Even though the setting sun was dim as it filtered through the thick cloud layer, the world around her was far brighter than it had been in the tunnels. She hadn't realized until now how used to the dark her eyes had grown.

Would it be like this in his mountain? Maladek tugged her forward, but she stumbled. She swiped at the tears blurring her vision every time she squinted her eyes open. Katie whispered an apology. "I can't see anything yet."

Without another word, he scooped her into his arms and began running. Memories of their first encounter played through her mind and made her chuckle into his chest. "At least I'm not tied up this time."

His warm pec rumbled with his smothered laugh. The air was humid and heavy here with a sweet stale smell that turned her stomach. Were they farther from the briny sea? After another few minutes, her eyes finally adjusted, and she peered around.

Sand, dull gray and depressing, stretched in every direction. Over his shoulder, she spotted a large, pointed castle rising in the distance. Other, shorter towers and buildings spotted the landscape all around it. Katie squinted and realized that the castle was formed with pieces of mismatched metal and black rock. The Sieliji had to use what they had on hand, she supposed. No one could accuse them of not recycling.

In the direction they were traveling stood a domed building, not much larger than a one-story house. Set a few yards apart was the cylindrical, pointed shaft of a rocket. It looked like a spacecraft that might have come from Earth, except the chipped writing on the side was in no lettering system she'd ever seen.

Maladek came to a halt behind a small dune that had formed in the sand and guided her to lie flat on her stomach behind it. "If I'm right, the Sieliji will be settling in for the night. We need to see how many barricade themselves in the communications station." He nodded toward the cylindrical rocket.

"What will you do?" she asked, a tremor in her voice fighting to undercut the confidence she feigned. "Do you think the fabric pieces will work in your ears? What if they have the control for your shock collar?"

Katie couldn't stop a tight, nervous feeling from skittering through her body. She'd only just found Maladek. The vision of a bright, happy future wavered in the forefront of her mind like a mirage. Though nothing had been settled between them, she couldn't let her newfound dream be torn away before she'd even had the chance to fight for it.

"They don't let prisoners come here. I only know about the beacon because when I landed the ship that brought me here, they directed us toward this spot. The guards have no reason to keep a control for my shock collar all the way over here."

Though Maladek's eyes remained focused on the buildings in front of them, Katie's kept flashing to him. "How many do you think will be in there?" The sharp blade Maladek had carved from the tunnel for her was heavy in her sweaty hand. She wiped her palm off on her robe.

"I doubt very many. It's unlikely any prisoner would be able to make it to the beacon above ground. The only way we were able to get here without running into patrolling Sieliji or quallie was because I knew how to navigate underground. They won't waste resources manning what they believe to be an unreachable station. I—"

His words were cut off, his body stiffening. He flipped to his back, hiding his protruding horns in the sand at the same time his hand flashed out to flatten her against the ground. While looking at the sky with a clenched jaw, he whispered,

"Tell me what they're doing. But be careful you aren't spotted."

Katie peeked over the top of the hill and spotted two Sieliji. One was exiting the small domed building while the other was exiting the rocket. "It looks like they're switching. There are two of them. But they look…" Katie's brows scrunched as she watched both Sieliji drag their feet and wobble. "Drunk," she finished. "Like they're about to fall over."

Maladek nodded, the movement causing sand to tumble down on his head as his horns jostled the little hill. "It's getting close to their hibernation time. They're able to wake up during the night if necessary, but it's as if they're half asleep. They're clumsy."

"Hopefully they won't be too hard to knock out, then."

Maladek made an uncertain rumble. "Even slow and half asleep, they're still faster than us on the sand."

Katie swallowed as the Sieliji both disappeared into their respective buildings. Perhaps they'd learned enough for one day. If she took too long to tell Maladek, maybe he'd decide to wait until tomorrow and they could crawl back into the safety of their tunnel. Clenching her jaw, Katie shook off the cowardly thoughts. "They've gone," she all but grated.

Before she'd built up enough courage to rise from the sands, Maladek had shot up, sweeping her into his arms before bolting toward the rocket. Katie's vision had returned, and she was more than capable of running, but she enjoyed being in his arms far too much to speak up.

He set her down in the sand a few feet away from the rocket and pulled his makeshift earplugs out of his pocket. They were made of the thin fabric of her underdress that he'd wrapped around some sticky mud so they'd be malleable. Katie kept her knife at the ready. If for whatever reason the earplugs didn't work, she'd need to attack the Sieliji on her own.

She flattened herself against the side of the rocket, out of sight, hoping that if the Sieliji did spot Maladek and if his earplugs failed, she might be able to catch the alien by surprise.

Maladek quietly positioned himself in front of the sturdy door and gripped the edges. His muscles tensing, he planted his feet apart. Stare determined, he took in a deep breath, then nodded at her. As soon as she nodded back, his body lurched backward, all his muscles straining to tear the metal from its hinges. The grip on her knife loosened for just a moment as she marveled once again at his strength. The metal groaned and cracked, then flew away from the building with a dull thud, sand spraying. Like a shot, he bolted into the room.

Ice slid down her spine, and her heartbeat thundered in her chest. At first there was only silence, but then she heard the screeching wail of the Sieliji. Her breaths were shaky and shallow, but Katie forced her eyes and ears to remain open and prayed the earplugs would work.

Finally, the Sieliji's piercing song faltered and then stopped entirely. Adrenaline had pins and needles slicing through her skin.

"Katie," Maladek's voice echoed from inside the room, and relief had her sucking in a breath. She rushed inside. The room was round, hollowed out from the inside, and crammed with towering piles of electronic parts. A technology hoarder's dream. She crept around the precarious piles until she spotted Maladek. He was fiddling with some controls on a long, rounded workspace. Mismatched screens and flickering lights on haphazardly welded-together panels stood away from the rest of the junk in the unbearably humid room.

A Sieliji lay crumpled face-up on the ground near a small cot, as if Maladek had thwacked him over the head as the creature was rousing from sleep. Maladek tore a piece of cloth from the bundle he'd stuffed into his pocket and tied it around the creature's mouth. He nodded toward the control panel and Katie rushed over, tiptoeing around the unconscious Sieliji. Disgust roiled in her already nervous belly at the image of his wide unblinking eyes.

Fear froze her in place. Her eyes remained glued to the Sieliji's until finally, its stillness told her it wasn't awake. She shuddered. *No eyelids.*

"Press this button. Hold it down and record a message to the royal family. Make sure to tell them your name, where we are, and that the prince is here." Maladek spoke a little too loudly, his muffled hearing making him unable to gauge his volume.

"Should I—" Katie stopped. If he couldn't hear that Sieliji's screech, it was unlikely he could hear her. She'd have to figure this out herself.

Maladek hefted the Sieliji under one arm, his attention darting to the entrance. "Hurry. He was fumbling with something on the control panel before I knocked him out. He may have alerted others. They'll be slow to rise, but we need to be ready to run. I'll keep watch outside."

Katie nodded and tried to tame all the thoughts racing through her mind. Oddly enough, this would be the most important voicemail she'd ever left. When Maladek was outside, she took a deep breath and held down the button.

"This message is for King Mistra and Queen Natihabe of the Endrolfen royal family. My name is Katherine Krauss. I work in the palace as a servant, and I was on the Myradium Galaxy cruise with Prince Skendro when our ship was brought down by Sieliji hunters. The survivors of the crash, the prince, and I are trapped on the Sieliji planet. I managed to escape capture, but the prince did not. The last I knew, the prince was alive."

It wasn't a lie, but it was misleading. The last she'd seen of the prince, he'd been in a lifeboat jettisoning away from their plummeting vessel. But she figured that information would only make the Endrolfen soldiers move slower. If they believed him to be alive, they'd come quickly. Katie held the button down for a moment longer, but didn't know what more there was to say. She finally finished with, "Please come soon and make sure to block your hearing. The prince was affected by the Sieliji song, and I assume all members of his species will also be affected."

Katie let go of the button. Her heart thrashed, crawling up her throat. The blinking and beeping of the screens in front of her remained unchanged. She wiped the sweat from her forehead and scanned the screens, looking for any sign her message had been sent.

"Maladek," she called, then remembered he couldn't hear her. She rushed out and found him prowling back and forth in front of the door. As she approached, his back stiffened, and he turned to face her. She nodded at him but motioned to the screens and lifted her hands in confusion. He stepped inside, angling his body sideways to avoid the precarious piles. Katie remained just inside the doorway, staring hard into the distance for any sign of reinforcements. Rustling from below her made her jerk and lose hold of her knife. She grappled to swipe it off the ground with her sweating palms and came face to face with the now conscious, wriggling Sieliji.

His pale eyes flashed up at her and the sharp, scalloped fins on the edge of his neck flared wide. Even though he didn't have eyebrows, or eyelids for that matter, Katie could tell he was livid. His piercing wail barely squeaked through the gag in his mouth. He dipped his head to his shoulder, trying to dislodge it, and she was finally jostled from her stupor. Katie brandished her knife, crouching down and holding it against his throat until he stilled.

She jumped when Maladek's vibrating footsteps sounded behind her, nerves on a razor's edge. His heavy palm landed on her shoulder and she rose, but didn't lower her knife. "It went through. Now we—"

Suddenly, a screech echoed in the distance, and Maladek thrust her behind him. She peeked out from behind his wide chest. The breath whooshed out of her body, throat going dry. Not one, but four Sieliji streamed out of the domed building.

Maladek uttered a curse and whirled her into his arms. He sprinted across the sand, but it was dryer than normal, and his progress was slowed as his feet sank into the sand with each pounding footfall.

Though Katie couldn't see them from her position in his arms, she knew the Sieliji were close. Their screeching calls pounded against her skull. She used Maladek's shoulders to lift herself and peer behind them and spotted all four Sieliji giving chase. Even though they wobbled and weaved as they ran, their hibernation slowing them, their wide webbed feet still ate up the sand much faster than any humanoid feet could.

Maladek stumbled then, and she fell back into his arms. Horror turned her bones to ice. His eyes were going in and out of focus. She stuffed her knife between her teeth and shoved her fingers into his ears, trying to stuff the plugs more firmly into place. But as the Sieliji neared, his steps slowed. Their screeching thundered across the sand, louder than anything she'd yet heard. All four together must be too much.

Katie wriggled, trying to get him to put her down. There had to be something she could do. At this pace, she could at least run as fast as him. His finger tightened around her, and he shook his head as though trying to dislodge something. He dropped her then and slammed his hands over his ears, snarling in frustration.

Katie tried to swallow past the hard knot in her throat. "Just listen to my voice, Maladek," she cried. She urged him forward with one hand on his arm. The other shook as she aimed the knife at their pursuers. Tears began to stream down her cheeks. The Sieliji were closing in, deadly swords and spears clutched in their hands.

A sob wrenched out of her throat when Maladek fell to his knees. "Run," he croaked.

A breath passed before Katie took in what his true meaning was. *Leave him to die.* The thought sobered her and spurred her to act. She ran. But not in the direction he'd intended. His anguished cry drifted on the air behind her as she ran not toward their underground hideout, but in the opposite direction—back toward the Sieliji outpost, making sure to sprint in a wide arc away from the guards.

She strained, pushing her legs to their limit. The muscles of her calves burned as her heels dug into the sand, swallowing her momentum. Her lungs heated and her breaths wheezed out of her. She chanced a glance over her shoulder and saw the Sieliji had paused, glancing first at Maladek and then at her.

Come on, you bastards. Follow me!

Finally, two broke off and raced after her. Her shout of victory remained buried beneath her deep, ragged inhales. She spotted Maladek and saw him shouldering off one screeching Sieliji. But the other dipped its head close and sang directly into his ear.

A strangled cry lodged in Katie's throat, vision blurring with renewed tears. Her inability to tear her gaze away from the man she loved made her stumble. She tripped, scraping her cheek against the rough sand as she slid to a stop. Her knife went flying, landing a few feet in front of her. Struggling toward it, she managed to grip the hilt just as a cold, moist hand clamped around her neck.

The Sieliji shrieked at her in that awful language and was midway through hauling her up when a loud, gurgling roar boomed all around them, shaking the ground and making the already unsteady Sieliji keel over. Their screeching stopped, the firm hold on her robe now lax. Scrambling to her feet, she whirled around, keeping her knees bent and brandishing her knife.

Katie shrieked, the sound an awful wail to rival any Sieliji song. Pale, fleshy pink and at least twelve feet tall, a quallie slithered toward them. The Sieliji behind her shoved her to the ground before running, leaving her as an offering in the path of the monstrous creature. The front of the quallie aimed at her was not round like a worm, but pointed like the edge of a pencil. Sharp, concentric circles of rocky scales spiraled around the length of its pointed nose, but she saw no mouth. No eyes. How would it kill her? Impale her?

She ran as fast as she could. The bone-chilling gurgling of the quallie pulsed under her skin. It was only a few feet away now; its roar echoed through the ground like an earthquake and made her stumble. The violent shuddering made her toe catch in the sand and she crashed to the ground. She turned on her back, crab-crawling away on one hand as she brandished the knife in the other.

The quallie was a foot away, the sharp tip of its nose rising. Her stomach roiled, and if she hadn't been so frozen with fear, she was sure she'd have vomited right there. The quallie's body lifted into the sky, and a disgusting slash on its underside opened into a writhing chasm of a mouth. It was going to swallow her whole.

As the quallie's mouth and body descended, ready to land directly over her, it jolted. Its movements grew jerky and unnatural. Like something was controlling it against its will. Then its massive body thundered to the ground before her, sand spraying upward in time with the impact.

12

aladek's fingers stabbed into the quallie's fleshy tail until his sharp knuckle plates pierced the skin; then he clenched the fatty layer underneath. Roaring to the sky, he yanked the beast as hard as he could, and it lurched toward him. The thick layers of fat and flesh were nothing compared to the strength that pulsed through him when he saw his mate about to be devoured.

He leaned back, digging all his weight into the sand with his heels, and dragged the writhing creature back one small footstep at a time. Its wretched howl shook the ground underfoot, but he only roared back. Nothing would hurt his female. Not as long as he had strength in his body. His muscles stretched beyond their limits. Something snapped in his arm, but he kept hauling the struggling creature back. His tendons might be tearing, his muscles pulling from his bones, but he felt no pain.

"Run, Katie," he bellowed. A flash of gray appeared as the quallie flapped its body back and forth. She sprinted in the direction of their tunnel, and the vise that had been crippling his chest finally loosened. Strength surged within him again. She was there. Alive!

One of the Sieliji he'd knocked out when the quallie first made its appearance had regained his senses. Now, he stood directly in her path. She spotted the Sieliji and angled herself to avoid running into him.

But then she glanced toward Maladek, and her pumping legs slowed. He kept his grip, but the quallie's flesh was tearing, and his fingers slid through slippery polyps of fat. He let out a roar as he struggled to hold on. His eyes never left Katie. The sight of her running to her freedom was the only thing keeping his body functioning. The Sieliji was wholly uninterested in Katie, its wide wet eyes focused on the flailing quallie.

Maladek's mate stared at him as he lost his hold of the slippery tail. He hurried to bury his fingers into a new spot, but his grip was weak. He could only command his hands to clench for so long before they stopped responding. Katie was about to pass the Sieliji, far closer than she should be. She glanced at the Sieliji and then at him and then at the quallie. To his shock, Katie charged for the dazed Sieliji.

The Sieliji was still staring at the quallie as he began to run, not paying Katie any mind. So when she smashed her blade into his shoulder, he let out a shriek of surprise and pain and toppled to the ground. She wrenched the blade out as the male fell, then continued sprinting toward their tunnel.

Maladek didn't immediately recognize the reason for her vicious display, but suddenly the quallie stilled, its body pivoting in the direction of the wounded Sieliji.

Understanding dawned. His beautiful, intelligent mate had given the quallie a new target. One it couldn't resist. A low rumbling reverberated through the ground as the quallie's long, pointed nose directed it toward the Sieliji and his delectable oozing blood. Maladek bolted, running to catch up with Katie while the quallie was distracted. The Sieliji had risen to his feet, running in the opposite direction and, by the goddess, the quallie was following his trail of pale blood.

Maladek didn't wait to see whether the Sieliji had gotten away, his focus totally consumed with his own target. Feeling her in his arms was the only thing he cared about. Katie let out a shriek when he caught up and lifted her over his shoulder without stopping. He couldn't make out exactly what she said, but he heard muffled sobs and felt her arms awkwardly circle around to his front, her cheek pressing against his back as though she were hugging him from her upside-down position.

He found the hole to their tunnel and whipped her off his shoulder, gently lowering her through. Then he dropped down. She'd scooped up the lantern they'd left near the entrance, but rather than stopping to gather his bearings, he tossed her over his shoulder and began running once more.

The most sickening terror he'd ever known quaked inside his bones, making his teeth grind and his mind blur with instinct. He needed to get her somewhere safe. Somewhere the Sieliji and quallie couldn't get to.

Noise, not as muffled as it had been a moment ago, buzzed through his head, and he distantly realized she'd taken out his earplugs. Though she spoke to him, he couldn't process her words. *Get her safe. Check her over.* He'd almost lost her.

The knowledge ripped him apart from the inside. Though he could feel her alive and warm under his palms, he couldn't seem to stop his heart from thrashing in his chest.

His knuckles scraped against the wall, making sparks fly as he searched for a hidden pocket to barricade them in. Finally, he found a small tunnel that led off in a direction they hadn't needed to go before. Not content with setting her down, he punched through the wall with his right hand, holding her tight in his shaky left arm.

The path opened, and he dashed through it. Then with no other option, he tilted her off his shoulder and tried to get his trembling hands to pile stone in front of the opening. He hacked at a large outcrop of rock and was satisfied when a pillar of stone broke away.

His palms sliced open as he roughly dragged the stone toward the sealed opening. He slammed the pillar against the piled stone cementing his work. No Sieliji could break through this. Not without him noticing.

He spun to Katie and could only stare. She stood stock still. Wide-eyed and skin leached pale, she stared back. Her breaths came in and out as fast as his.

"Are you okay?" she asked in a shaky whisper. Her gaze traveled down to his hands.

A faint drip hit his ears then, and he peered down at his cut palms. His own blood mixed with the grease of the quallie blubber. Disgust and the memory of the beast looming over his Katie had him dragging his sore palms over his pants.

All at once, emotion overcame him. His breaths quaked out of him, and his eyes watered as he kept them wide, unable to look away from her even to blink. Maladek wilted, falling to his knees.

Katie rushed to him with a whimper, but before she could join him on the ground, he wrapped his arms around her legs and pressed her lower body into his chest, burying his face just above her belly. His arms shook as he tried not to grip her too tightly.

The acrid scent of fear and Sieliji scum clung to the rough fabric of her robe, and he fumbled with the stays holding it together and tore it open. He pressed his face into her soft underdress, inhaling deeply, taking her scent into his lungs. Fear still clung to her skin, and Maladek held her more tightly.

He didn't know how long he stayed there, but after a while he became aware of the sensations of her fingers raking through his hair and her arm looped around his head, holding him close.

"We're okay. I'm okay," she cooed.

She wiggled in his embrace, and he finally had enough awareness to loosen his hold. When he did, she knelt and took his head between her palms. He gazed into her worried eyes. The light blue looked even paler against the irritated red of her whites.

Katie brushed her thumb over his brow. "Are you okay?" she asked again.

Maladek didn't know what came over him, but in that moment, all he knew was that she was his. She needed to know. "You're my mate, Katie," he croaked.

Her brows furrowed and her fingers stopped. His hands automatically rose and wrapped around her forearms. His palms stung, but her reaction was the only thing he could focus on. A new type of dread settled in his gut when she remained silent.

"Your mate? You want to ask me to be your mate?" Her brows were still furrowed, and she tipped her head to the side as if she were concerned that he'd had a head injury and didn't know what he was saying.

Maladek lifted his hands to her face, spreading his fingers so she could see the curling purple designs. "You *are* my mate. The one chosen by the goddess. We were fated to find each other here. My marks appeared as soon as I scented you in the trench. When you almost…" He faltered, throat going tight "You must understand. If you had not survived, I would not survive. I will follow you anywhere, Katie. Whether it be to Betuhines, to Earth, to the afterlife. Our souls are bound."

Sadness briefly dimmed her eyes. "You mean you have no choice in the matter? You're tied to me whether you want to be or not."

His incredulous bark of laughter made her jump. "I have wanted you from the moment I saw you digging through that scrap pile. I've admired your loyalty and your beauty and your kindness since my instincts forced me to carry you away. I'm tied to you because you are the missing part of me, and I you. Divine intervention has merely put you in my path, but I was always waiting for you. I fear the only one who may not have a choice is you. I can't let you go, Katie. You told me that you didn't belong anywhere, that you felt alone. Do you still feel that way with me?"

Katie's expression remained blank as she stared at him. Maladek barely managed to keep his grip on her arms from tightening.

Then, the corner of her mouth lifted, and his heart skipped. He tried to keep his emotions in check. To not celebrate quite yet. But when her wide, sparkling smile ignited across her face, he couldn't keep the purr from rumbling through him.

"No, I don't. I feel…right when I'm with you." Her smile warmed his insides, loosening bunched tension.

"I know I could make you happy in time," he pressed, not wanting to give her any reason to second-guess her words.

Her hands moved from his cheeks to drape over his shoulders. She leaned toward him. "You've made me happy in the bowels of a horrific planet with nothing but a survival pack and your company. I've never felt more connected to anyone in my life. Even if you left me after we were saved, I would've treasured these few days with you. I think…" She inhaled, her expanded chest brushing across his. Her brows furrowed, as if she couldn't quite believe her own words. "I think I'm in love with you."

His purr thundered out of him, bouncing off the stone walls. His nose delved into the curve of her neck, inhaling her bright, sweet scent. "I love you too."

13

Maladek had spent the last three days exploring Katie and was floored to find that she welcomed all his advances. She'd accepted him. Accepted their bond. He could scarcely force himself to sleep each night for fear he'd wake to find she'd simply been a vision forced into his brain by the Sieliji.

But when he woke with her wrapped in his arms each morning, purple mating marks glowing bright against her pale skin, his beaming smile couldn't be kept from his face.

That first morning, he'd kept her in his eyeline as he'd dug out their barricade. Embarrassment had heated his cheeks all the way to his horns when he'd realized he barreled through the walls, locking them in before grabbing their packs. He never wanted to feel that fear again. That numbing, all-encompassing terror.

A quiet dread still lingered underneath his bliss, however. What would happen when the Betuhinians came? What if they took her away from him? What if they decided she was theirs, after all? Who in their right mind wouldn't love her? He found his grip on her tightening whenever these thoughts entered his mind. So when the distant, almost imperceptible rumbling from above told him a large ship had arrived, he'd argued with himself whether to tell her.

His internal debate had been absurd and short-lived. Their dwindling rations and her worn clothing made the choice for him. He was also sure he'd torn something in his shoulder during their fight, and though the pain didn't bother him, not being at peak strength in case he needed to protect his mate again did.

Katie's eyes widened when he gently roused her and told her the cavalry had arrived. Her bright, beaming grin infected him down to his marrow. Being the one to make her light up like that, even if he wasn't precisely the cause, was the most satisfying thing he'd ever experienced. No wonder the old carved tales lining his mountain's halls described mates surmounting impossible feats for one another. If Katie told him she was thirsty, he was quite sure he could carve a river with his horns if necessary.

Maladek couldn't keep the knot in his gut from tightening as he emerged from their tunnel and took stock of the situation above ground. Hordes of Sieliji barreled out of their city in the distance, heading for the sleek, golden Betuhinian ship which had landed in the exact coordinates Maladek had attached to Katie's message. Though they had large numbers, the Sieliji attack on the vast Endrolfen vessel was laughable.

Katie and Maladek watched from a safe distance as the Betuhinian army, complete with the king himself, emerged in shining golden armor wielding laser weapons that the Sieliji's paltry blades would have no chance against. By the time the sun was halfway overhead, the Sieliji forces had been subdued.

Maladek and Katie shuffled toward the ship, hands aloft in surrender, and were met by a small contingent. Maladek remained stiff as stone, crowding against Katie as much as possible while they were shuttled back to the ship. These people were not the enemy, yet his instincts wouldn't allow him to relax, even when Katie swept her soft hand up and down his forearm to soothe him.

When they arrived at the ship, a few Betuhinians recognized Katie, the queen included. A small bit of Maladek's tension lifted when he saw them give his mate the sincere, grateful thanks she deserved. She was the only reason their son was alive—or at least had made it to the planet alive.

As Katie and Maladek were taken to the medical bay and fixed up, smaller transport vessels skimmed over the planet, looking for prisoners. To Maladek's relief, they freed every single one they came across rather than leaving them to their fate in favor of finding the prince. Katie wanted to remain outside, but he managed to convince her to change clothes and eat first. He scowled when, after taking only a couple bites of food and gulping down a cup of water, she dashed back outside, Maladek hot on her heels.

Katie refused to leave the entry bay as groups of wide-eyed prisoners were loaded onto the Endrolfen ship. Maladek didn't mind.

Though he'd prefer to whisk her to a safe room and wait out the search away from curious eyes and the scowling, bound Sieliji, he adored the way she clung to him, unconsciously squeezing his hand in anxious excitement every time a new transport delivered a load of rescued prisoners.

She didn't seem to notice the critical gaze of her Betuhinian friends, either. They stared at his scraped, scarred skin and uneven horns while ruffling their pristine, shining feathers. Even though the Betuhinians were tall, many as tall as him even, they were delicate things. Brittle and elegant. He was as far from their version of idealized beauty as you could get.

Maladek thrust his shoulders back and ignored them. He wasn't used to feeling so self-conscious, and Katie's ignorance of their disapproval helped to soothe his nerves. But what would happen when she finally calmed and noticed how her adopted family viewed him? Would she change her mind? Would her opinion of him shift? He knew in his heart she wasn't so fickle, but this sudden insecurity was a hard thing to ignore.

He pulled her against him, wrapping his arms around her front as her stiff back pressed into his chest. She nestled against him instantly, and a ragged, relieved purr rumbled through his chest.

* * *

Where was Char Tomi? Why hadn't they found him yet? And where was the prince? He was the most important person of all. The blessedly thorough Betuhinians had brought back hundreds of prisoners so far and every transport-load had Katie's stomach roiling with dread. The only thing holding her together was Maladek's strong, unfaltering presence.

My mate. A thrill ran through her, briefly snuffing out the anxiety.

The sun dipped close to the horizon. It was time to retreat into the ship for the night. The search would be called off until the next morning, yet she couldn't make herself go inside. The last boat of the day glided to a stop in front of the Endrolfen vessel and her fingers tightened around Maladek's solid arms, circling her.

She peered over at the king and queen, who had not moved from their watchful spot outside, either. Her heart ached for them. Though they were adept at hiding it, Katie could see the pain and worry in their expressions. The set of their fluffy brows was a little too low. Their regal, board-stiff postures a little too limp.

A gaggle of twittering physicians and attendants erupted from the transport, and Katie froze. The king and queen sped toward their son with high-pitched warbles as the prince hobbled out of the boat. His fringed frock was all but rags, bright pieces of pink and orange fringe falling here and there and exposing sunburned flesh. The feathers on his eyebrows and head were spotty and plucked as though he'd molted. Without thinking, Katie rushed forward, but had the wind knocked out of her with a huff when the band of Maladek's arm remained in place.

She squirmed and looked up at his face to find his jaw stiff and brows furrowed. "Come on," she said. "Let me go. I need to see if he knows what happened to Char Tomi." Maladek surveyed the crowd twice before finally loosening his grip. She dashed toward the prince, but was stopped short by a guard's outstretched arm.

A vicious growl broke behind her. Maladek had been kept even farther away than her. He glared not at his three guards, but at hers, his fists clenching. She held up a hand to him and though his expression didn't soften, he didn't push through the guards surrounding him, their wary eyes taking him in as their fingers fiddled with their weapons.

When Katie turned back, the prince's eyes found hers. He swept his hands to either side, and like magic, a path opened in the crowd. He crossed to her and placed both palms on her shoulders. The prince rarely, if ever, noticed her, and this focused physical display had her shoulders hitching.

"You were the one who saved me?" the prince said. "You dragged me to that pod, and I'm told you are the one who evaded the Sieliji and sent a distress signal to my family?"

The words were more a statement than a question, but Katie nodded anyway. "Maladek, my mate, also helped. I couldn't have done any of it without him." Katie pointed him out. The faintest flinch lit the prince's face at her unsung words, but he hid his reaction quickly, and his gaze traveled to where she'd pointed. When he caught sight of Maladek, his sparse brows rose. He nodded to the guards, and they stepped away from Maladek. At any other time, the relief on their faces at not having to contend with her edgy mountain of a man would have been hilarious.

As soon as they'd stepped away, Maladek was at her side in a flash.

"I owe you my life, Katherine Krauss, and you, Maladek. Please tell me if there's anything I can ever do for you." Katie had the oddest realization then. The grumpy man currently staring daggers at the prince's hands on her shoulders was all she'd ever want in the world. The knowledge warmed her heart.

"I'd like to leave your service, if you'd allow it." As respectfully as she could, she shuffled out of the prince's hold and into Maladek's waiting arms. "I'd like to travel back to my mate's home planet."

"That is no favor. You're free to leave, of course. And if you ever require anything else, you need only call." The prince tilted his head back and warbled a beautiful melody into the sky. Katie's cheeks and forehead heated as the crowd of Betuhinian onlookers all craned their necks and joined in. The royal song was reserved for heroes. The highest honor a citizen could receive. She didn't feel quite deserving enough of such recognition.

She was about to say just that when a tall, golden figure emerged from the transport. He stumbled out, looking much more slight than she remembered, and their gazes met. Katie tried as hard as she could to keep her attention on the prince. This was the highest honor, after all.

Either bravery or arrogance had the prince reaching out to grip both Maladek and Katie's shoulders. He gave them both a small squeeze and a warm smile, then released them and dashed back over to his parents, who twittered their own loving song as they embraced him.

Katie pulled out of Maladek's hold with a reassuring squeeze and rushed toward Char Tomi. In a flash, he was next to her. Physical intimacy was only common in the rarest of instances, and even now Katie was surprised when Char Tomi threw his arms around her. A distant snarl sounded from a few feet behind her, but she ignored it. Her mate was prickly, but she somehow knew he wouldn't interfere unless he had to.

"I'm so happy you're okay," she cried, pressing her cheek into Char Tomi's narrow chest.

His body tensed, and his familiar voice echoed in her head. *I'm also very grateful that you're alive, Katie. But do you know there is a very large, very angry male staring at us?*

Katie chuckled and pulled back, swiping her happy tears away. "Yes." She tugged Char Tomi over to Maladek, who'd pulled himself up to his full height, the muscles of his arms bulging. His narrowed gaze focused on her hand, still gripping Char Tomi's arm.

"Maladek, this is my best friend, Char Tomi. Maladek helped me find you," Katie added when the two men only glared at each other. Char Tomi's eyes swirled with pink, but Katie heard nothing. Though Char Tomi could allow her to hear whatever he said as well, it seemed he was speaking only to Maladek. She frowned and glanced between the men. She studied her mate's expression and saw it darken, the corners of his eyes veining with black.

She smacked Char Tomi on the shoulder. "What did you say to him? Be nice."

Char Tomi ignored her, and his eyes swirled again. A low warning rumbled through Maladek's throat. She flattened her palm on his chest as if that could hold him back if he really wanted to get to Char Tomi.

"I know," Maladek growled in response to whatever Char Tomi had said.

She looked closely at her friend and saw his eyes had widened in surprise. Whatever he'd said, Char Tomi hadn't expected Maladek's response. His gaze bounced between her and Maladek, then without warning, he grabbed her arm and flashed them away. The world spun, then jolted on its axis when Char Tomi finally stopped. She always hated running with him. It was so disorienting.

Do you know what he did, Katie? Char Tomi asked in a rush as she tried to bring the world back into focus.

"What are you talking—" A distant roar built in volume, and she twirled. Maladek was currently barreling toward them, eyes black and features enraged. "Crap! Why did you do that? He's going to kill you, you idiot." Katie watched her mate as he flew over the sand, holding one hand to her head and the other on her hip. How was she going to keep the man she loved from ripping apart her best friend?

Before she could figure it out, Char Tomi grabbed her and flashed to the opposite side of the ship.

"Stop it!" Katie yelled while tripping over her own feet. Char Tomi caught her before she tumbled to the ground.

He's not worthy of you. Did he tell you how he ended up here? Those of us who weren't affected by the Sieliji talked while we worked. They told me about him. He—

"Yes! I know how he ended up here. He told me. He explained it all." Katie glared at Char Tomi. "Did they also tell you about how he kept me safe and alive for the last few days?" Katie pushed on Char Tomi's chest. Her irritation with her friend grew when she spotted Maladek stampeding toward them in the distance. "Did they tell you that he tunneled through miles of sharp rock to help me find your ungrateful ass? Did they tell you that he as good as sacrificed his life to save me from not one, but four Sieliji *and* a quallie?"

Char Tomi's eyes widened for a moment before narrowing stubbornly. His irises began to swirl, but before he could answer, Katie held up a hand.

"No, they didn't because they haven't actually ever met him, have they? I appreciate your concerned big brother act, but you could have talked to me about this in a million different ways and you know you only chose to do it like this to rile him up." Char Tomi's voice started up in her head again, but Katie pushed on. "Now, go get to the med bay before he gets a hold of you, and I'll try to figure out a way to smooth this over."

Char Tomi didn't move. He stared, and after a moment, spoke in her head. *You seem certain.* A slight smile lifted the corner of his mouth.

Katie chuckled. "I am, you great golden idiot. I love him."

Char Tomi glanced at her livid hulking hero, still much too far away to reach them in time if Char Tomi decided to whisk her away again. *I'm struggling to see why.*

"You will." She gave him a hard pinch and laughed again. "Now get out of here."

Char Tomi turned to face Maladek with a raised chin, then flashed away. Maladek's gaze followed, but he continued to barrel toward her instead, though his murderous expression told her he wanted to pursue her friend.

When he finally got to her, his chest heaved in massive breaths and he lifted her against his chest, squeezing almost too tight. "Calm down," Katie crooned. "Char Tomi was just being an overprotective idiot."

"I'll kill him if he does that again." Her feet dangled as he stomped toward the ship, still clutching her as though Char Tomi would pop up any second and steal her away.

Katie struggled to pull back, and after an argumentative tightening of his arms, he let her. "You will not. He's my family, and you two will have to learn to get along." Maladek's brows were still drawn, something other than anger creeping beneath his tight expression. "Put me down."

Slowly, he let her slide down his body.

"What did he say to you?" she asked, reaching up to force his gaze to hers instead of the ship.

When he finally looked at her, the hard line between his brows relaxed. "He…he told me he knew what I'd done. He said I didn't deserve you."

Katie's brain replayed the brief silent exchange the two men had had, and she frowned. "You said 'I know.' I remember that's how you answered him. 'I know.'"

Maladek's jaw tensed. "I don't deserve you, but I refuse to give you up. I'll spend every day of my life working to be good enough for you, if that's what it takes."

With her grip on his face, she pulled him toward her. "You are more than good enough for me. You're perfect, and I wouldn't change a thing about you, just as you wouldn't change a thing about me, right?"

She could see her words soothe the buried worry he'd been keeping inside. A lazy grin spread as his limbs became more pliant before her eyes. "I might make you a little less likeable if I had my way. It'd be easier to keep you to myself if you were unlikeable."

"Is that right?" Katie grinned.

Maladek let out a sigh and pulled her close. "No. I'd change nothing."

"See? We belong together, like you said. Nothing will ever change that. I've never felt more myself than when I'm with you. So let whatever doubts you've been keeping inside go. You're mine now. Forever."

"Your prisoner, am I?" Maladek teased, pressing a soft, toe-curling kiss to her lips that smothered her chuckle. "To have you as my jailor is the most exquisite punishment."

Maladek pulled away, gazing down into her eyes and pinching one bedraggled curl. Katie's heartbeat fluttered at the deep tenderness shining back, which undercut his playful words.

"My heart already belongs to you, Katie. Love is not a strong enough word, but I love you with everything I have."

Tears pricked the corners of her eyes, emotion clogging her throat. Unable to form words through the blazing happiness flaring in her soul, she kissed him again and thanked all the gods she knew of that she'd been led to Maladek.

14

Katie fiddled with her hair again. For over a week, she and Maladek had been surrounded by people. The ship that had rescued them from the Sieliji planet had been a joyful place, and no one was more eager to express their renewed verve for life than Prince Skendro. He grinned eagerly and mingled with the rescued prisoners as if they were old friends. He was a changed person.

Knowing of hardship and experiencing it were very different, and the prince displayed a sense of empathy and camaraderie she'd never seen him show towards strangers. Though his parents wanted him back on Betuhines as soon as possible, he pressed for them to deliver each and every prisoner to their home world using the rescue vessel. Any argument for placing them on a ship of their own while the royal family returned to Betuhines fell on deaf ears.

And if the prince treated all the strangers on the ship as friends, he treated Katie and Maladek as nothing less than heroes. Between Prince Skendro constantly seeking them out, Char Tomi driving Maladek up a wall with his telepathic conversation and critical gaze, and the daily celebrations, she and her mate had been hard pressed to find time alone. Already transporting a small army, they couldn't even find a moment's peace at night as everyone was forced to share sleeping quarters.

But now, finally, they were alone in a cruiser, minutes from arriving at his home city of Tetranica, yet instead of reveling in the blessed privacy with her mate, all she could do was worry.

When her palm lifted to brush over her hair again, Maladek snatched her wrist, then squeezed her hand in his. He'd been quiet as well, a muscle working in his jaw.

"Sorry," she said. "It's weird not wearing my headdress. I feel naked."

"I can source a new cover for your hair before we enter the city if it'd make you more comfortable." He smiled down at her, though his eyes trailed up to her hair after a moment as if he were trying to take in the last views of a glorious sunset before it disappeared.

Despite the worry gnawing at her insides, a flutter started up in her belly. She could relate to the adoring looks he always leveled on her. He seemed to grow more handsome with each day that passed, so much so that she found herself holding her breath in the morning right before she opened her eyes to see him. His injuries were healed, his hair clean and trimmed, and his large muscular body had shockingly filled out even more, helped along by the piles of food he ate every meal.

Today his wide shoulders were hidden under a fine smokey gray coat, and his dark hair was braided back between his horns. Even though his tamed appearance made her heart skip a beat, it was odd to see him like this. Almost unrecognizable from the rough man she'd survived with in those caves. It was as if they'd been torn from one painting and plopped into another of a completely different style. They were still them, but they didn't quite fit yet.

"Do you think your people will like me?" she whispered. Her palm buried under his twitched as she tried to toy with her hair again. The tension in his jaw relaxed somewhat as his ruby eyes turned toward her. The palm he lifted to cup her cheek was soft and warm against her skin. No trace of the rough cuts from only a week ago.

"Is that what you've been worried about, love?"

"Haven't you?" she asked with a half-smile. "I can tell you've been anxious too."

Maladek grinned down at her. "I've been working hard to ensure everything is prepared for your arrival and it's been stressful not to be able to set up the house myself. Never for an instant have I been concerned with my people not loving you. Though, I hope you won't mind me keeping you to myself for a few days before I introduce you to my family."

Katie flushed. A little of her anxiety ebbed at his words, just like it always did. "I'd love that."

"Good." Maladek wrapped his arm around her waist and hoisted her onto his lap, pressing her close. "Shall we stop harboring secret worries from each other then?"

Katie nodded and buried her face in the crook of his neck, pressing a kiss to his pulse point that made him purr.

"Careful female, unless you want me to redirect this cruiser to take a tour of the mountain range."

With a grin, she sat up. "No, I want to see your home. I'm curious to know if it's how I pictured."

His mouth twitched down. "*Our* home," he corrected seriously. Before she could agree, the cruiser pulled to a stop, and she scrambled off his lap. Half her life in the palace had been spent making sure she was either presentable or unseen and she wouldn't have his people's first view of her to be straddling one of their own.

As it turned out, she needn't have worried. The cruiser door slid open, letting in a gust of warm air and revealing a lit cavern with imposing carved stone doors. Maladek exited the cruiser first, then helped her out, before pulling her toward the entrance to his home city. He kept her hand wrapped within his as they waited for the towering doors to swing inward.

Adapting to a new planet wouldn't be easy. From experience she knew the next few years would be rife with missteps and cultural misunderstandings, but she'd done it before, and by all the gods she could do it again. She glanced up at Maladek, whose hopeful, concerned gaze was fully focused on her and knew that it would be different this time. She wasn't alone anymore. She had him. Her mate.

Every nerve lodged in her throat like a softball as the doors groaned apart and Katie waited for her first view of Tetranica.

* * *

Maladek watched Katie take in the cavernous entry hall of his home city, and let the familiar scents and sounds fill an empty space in his chest he hadn't acknowledged. Dozens of behemoth stone pillars circled a raging central fire and stretched up toward the arched ceiling far above. Curls tumbled over Katie's shoulders as she craned her neck back as far as she could and stared at the scenes sculpted above.

Tetran ancestors, fifty times the size of Maladek, had been carved into the ceiling to appear as if they were clawing their way free from the warm, brown stone. Their spiraling horns pointed down at the passersby like deadly stalactites as the light from the fire below flickered off their faces.

This area of the mountain had been carved centuries ago, chosen because of the rich jewel deposits. As his ancestors had excavated, they'd used talented artists to sculpt every available surface, utilizing the glittering gem's deposit placement to enhance their work and pay homage to the natural structure of the mountain, rather than mining the gems and placing them in the works of art. The effect was deep outcroppings of precious stones mixed with carved

Tetrans that told stories. Their life on the old planet. The settling of the new planet.

Maladek's favorite piece, the largest of all, stood on the other side of the entry in a solid wall of rock. A colossal figure of the goddess loomed naked and imperious as she surveyed her city far below. Her left hand was held in front of her round belly, and she cradled a mountain range in her upturned palm. Raised high above her head, her right hand stretched to a horizontal slash of gems. Bright blue, purple, and yellow crystals sparkled in the expansive outcropping and gave the illusion the goddess was holding up the sky itself while protecting their mountains in her womb.

The central hearth burned brightly, warming the room and making the cavern's crystals sparkle on all sides. Firelight set Katie's face and hair aglow as her wide eyes scanned every inch of the space in awe. "This place is…" Katie shook her head and swallowed, searching for the right words. "Impossible."

Maladek chuckled and guided her forward. He'd only had the pleasure of seeing a newcomer's reaction to Tetranica a few times in his life, but the sheer astonishment on their faces never got old. The entry hall was a hand carved wonder.

Shops lined the perimeter of the space and the pillars, while high arched hallways led to the maze of passages that curled through the mountain range. Curious stares landed on Katie, and he was suddenly impatient to get her to their house before anyone caught sight of his marked hands and bombarded them with questions and congratulations. There would be time enough to celebrate the fact he'd returned to Tetranica a mated male. For now, all he wanted was to get her into their home. To have her energy and her scent fill the space until even the stone recognized her presence.

He led Katie through the crowds toward one of the transport stations, then seated them both in the plush round car. She gripped his thigh when he programmed the car to rise to the third level of the mountain and jettison them toward the neighboring peak. The car sped through narrow passageways past glittering mines, springs with steam rising off their pools, and crowded markets, until he came to their stop before a heavy metal door, which unlocked and slid open at his arrival.

Once they stepped through the threshold, their car raced away, heading to the next nearest station and Maladek let out a relieved breath. "We're home," he whispered. Long damp nights spent in his damp cell on Sielijia had almost convinced him he'd never see this place again.

"Wow," Katie breathed, a grin firmly in place on her face.

His chest expanded at her appreciation. He couldn't wait to show her more. The entryway was a wide hallway leading off to their right and left. In front of them, two staircases led down a short distance into a seating area filled with low comfortable furniture, all pointing toward the floor to ceiling stretch of windows that gave a spectacular view of the valley beyond. The peaks were mostly bare now. Too cold for the bright green grass that covered the valley in summer, but too warm for snow to blanket the world outside in white.

He explored the upper floor with her, first showing her the wife's quarters. He'd taken time on their weeklong journey home to ensure the space was furnished before they arrived and was relieved that Biroun, who'd insisted on seeing to all the work, had come through for him. A large fluffy mattress, the softest money could buy, took up an entire corner of the room and was surrounded on two sides by windows, which gave a slightly different view of the valley, and overlooked a waterfall.

The carved walls, bleached a lighter shade of brown, were inset with fine blue stones as if he'd known that his future love would have eyes of the same color when he'd been commissioning the work. Maladek was also pleased to see Biroun had piled every bare surface of the room with the bridal gems Maladek had mined for decades.

His Katie squealed, a sound that put him on high alert for only a moment until he realized it was a high-pitched warble of happiness. She knelt and admired a yellow stone as tall as her shin.

"They're yours to do with as you wish," he explained, not able to keep the grin from his face. Pride and joy at seeing her happy because of something he'd provided almost made him lightheaded.

"You found all these?" she asked with an impressed lift of her brows that made his smile widen.

"I found most right over there," he pointed toward a shorter mountain in the distance that many of his people had overlooked because of its size and crumbling exterior.

She plucked one clear stone from atop a shelf and held it upright above one of her fingers. "I think the girls from my high school would keel over if they saw a wedding ring with a rock this size. What do you think?" she asked, a joking twitch to her lips.

Stepping behind her, he wrapped his arms around her waist as she continued to admire the stone. "I think I'd have to hold your arm up for you it would be so heavy."

She chuckled, replaced the stone, and turned in his arms. Maladek couldn't comprehend it, but the gaze she leveled on him was more admiring and covetous than any she'd laid on the riches in the room around her. As if *he* were the real prize.

"Let me show you my quarters next, then we can tour the lower level." Her fingers stilled as they twirled a lock of his hair at his nape.

"Is it common to have separate quarters?" Her lips thinned more than normal, though he could tell she was trying to appear casual.

"They do," he said, an unspoken question in his voice.

"On Earth, couples share rooms." She shrugged, eyes moving to his chest as if the comment were of no importance.

Maladek's heart pounded, his fingers on her hips curling tighter. "You wish to share your space with me?"

"I mean…only if you want to. I'm sure it won't be a problem if we have our own rooms, but I didn't know if it was important to you or not. I mean I guess I can see the benefit of having our own spaces." Her eyes drifted around her room curated with comfortable furs and stuffed with priceless jewels, and yet a crease formed between her brows.

"I would chain you to my side and never spend a moment away from you if it were up to me, my beautiful Katie," he whispered, recapturing her attention.

She gave a tentative smile. Her eyes flashed up to his. "Really?" she asked, biting her lip to hold back a grin. "You're sure?"

Maladek tried not to scoff. To have access to her all night? To run his palms over her curves and feel her body tucked against his and wake up with her scent heavy in his lungs? The only thing more wonderful than that thought was the knowledge she wanted it as well.

"Shall we go cause a cave-in in my old quarters so I can prove it to you?" Though it was a joke, if she requested it, he'd tear apart his room and bury the contents at the mere hint it would make her happy.

"That won't be necessary," she smiled.

"You know…there is one *other* room I'm particularly eager to show you." He dipped his head to Katie's neck and inhaled. A purr rumbled through his throat.

15

Katie tried to keep her fingers from shaking with excitement. She was about to drink vishou, an act held sacred by her mate. She'd been imagining this day since he'd first told her about the ritual, yet as she watched Maladek grind a slice of his horn to dust, she wondered which of them was more excited.

His eyes, now veined with black, remained glued to her as he worked the jewel encrusted crystal pestle in the matching mortar. Katie eyed the bulging veins and muscles of his forearm and heat built low in her belly.

Was it a good idea to try this when they'd been forced to go so long without sex? She needed to cool her desire, or she may explode when the potent aphrodisiac took hold.

She inhaled a calming breath and forced herself to study her surroundings instead of the sexy man in front of her. The vishlouti room was different than she'd imagined, but better too. There were no windows here, the room having been built in the lowest level of the house, deep in the mountain. Instead, the space was lit by small radiant orbs that floated around the ceiling like giant fireflies and cast everything in a sultry glow.

Unlike every other wall she'd seen in Tetranica so far, these walls weren't made of stone. They were covered in padded panels of plum fabric and embroidered with silvery green stitching.

The only bit of rock she *could* see was an extraordinary mosaic of black and white stone bordering the perimeter of the room. Apart from that narrow band of hard walkway, the room was adorned with furnishings designed for comfort. Soft cushions sprawled over the floors amid low tables and long padded benches. A wide mattress dominated the back wall. Even the ceiling was draped in expensive textiles, giving the room the impression of seclusion and intimacy.

It was quiet and subtle perfume lingered in the air just enough to make Katie feel lazy but not tired. The dark colors of the walls and the trapped warmth radiating from heavy fabric cocooned them. But rather than feel claustrophobic, she felt safe. Katie now understood why Maladek had hiked her over his shoulder and carried her off to the caves back on Sielijia.

"Are you nervous, little mate?" Maladek purred, sending a sizzle of electricity down her spine.

Her breaths grew shallow as she watched him pour the powder into a crystal goblet and mix it with dark liquid. "Yes." There was no use in denying it. She was excited and impatient and yet still nervous.

He centered the glass in front of her on their low jade table and sat back. His smile was tender, as though her honesty warmed him. "We don't have to do this now, love."

The words were like a punch to her senses, dissolving any reservations lingering in her mind. Without hesitation, Katie lifted the inky black vishou to her mouth, met Maladek's ruby gaze, and drank. The corners of his eyes crinkled, his warm grin turning hungry as she drained the glass.

The liquid wound a heated path down her throat. Goosebumps pricked to life on her skin.

Maladek reclined with one palm behind him. He watched her the way a silent predator watches its prey unwittingly wander too close. Hungrily. Greedily. Yet oh so patiently.

Something in her turned wicked at his restrained expression. In a few minutes, she'd be overcome with desire and if she was going to ache for him, she'd make sure he ached for her too.

Katie let her mouth curl into a sultry smile. "You taste good," she crooned before licking her lips.

A choked sound escaped her mate, his jaw dropping as he let out a rough breath. She rose to her knees and began crawling toward him.

"You know, you said something to me back in the caves that I haven't forgotten." She loved the way his chest rose and fell more quickly the closer she got. "There's a certain luxury you said you'd accept only when we were clean, safe, and back in your home."

By the time she arrived between his bent knees, Maladek's eyes were suffused in black, and the ghost of a growl lingered on his deep exhales. The smell and heat of him drifted over her like silk. She couldn't hold back an unbidden sigh. Was the vishou taking effect even now?

"Will you let me taste more of you?" She grinned.

He stopped her when she reached for the stays of his pants and spoke in a rasp. "I should be touching you, working you up until you beg for my cock, not…not taking from you."

Katie beamed at her glorious male. He was always so generous, trying to turn her down even though the pained expression and tensed jaw told her it was an arduous battle. She melted against his chest and kissed him.

The vishou was definitely working its way through her system now. The feel of his soft lips under hers was heightened. The sensations—his taste, the heat of his tongue, the firm pressure of his palms still clutched protectively around her wrists—they were enough to make her dizzy. She moaned and pulled away, determined to reach her goal before the vishou took control of her sense entirely.

She pinned him with a fierce gaze. "I *am* begging, Maladek."

***

By the goddess, how was he supposed to withstand words like that? And when they were said in her sweet voice, gone husky with need? Maladek could move mountains with his hands, but he wasn't strong enough for this. "I can deny you nothing, little mate."

As soon as his palms on her wrists had loosened, she tore at the fastenings of his pants, then dragged them off his legs. He slipped his shirt over his head and basked in her scorching gaze as her eyes roamed over his chest and slipped down to his stiff shaft.

Her movements were shaky as she lowered herself toward his lap. It was clear the vishou was pulsing through her now, her desire building. He could scent it in the air and see it in the dilation of her pupils.

But though the vishou was heightening her pleasure and her eagerness, Maladek remained just as affected. His body was on fire, his brain cycling through every depraved position he wanted to take her in.

He'd always thought when he got his mate back into his vishlouti that he'd take his time, strip her slowly while letting her heightened senses cause her to shiver with delight. But now? His mind was a dark mess of selfish thoughts.

He'd never taken this pleasure before, only learning it was common to her species after some interesting reading on the ship. Maladek must be the greediest male on the planet, for all he wanted was to know what her pink tongue would feel like running along the ridges of his shaft and how soft the warm wet curves of her mouth would feel sliding over him.

So, shamefully, when her warm breath ghosted over the head of his cock, he didn't pull her away. He hissed in a breath, balled his hands into fists at his sides, and waited to see what she'd do next.

Always surprising him, his lovely human didn't do what he expected, though. She didn't give him a tentative lick or run her palm over him gently first. She descended as though starved, taking him deep and moaning out a rumbling sound of pleasure. It took everything in Maladek not to buck his hips or bury his fingers in her hair. But the bellow he let out couldn't be helped.

Tremors running through his muscles kept him anchored to his body as she slid her glistening lips up and down his shaft, while her nails dug into the sides of his thighs as though she were ensuring he remained in place for her mind-numbing ministrations. As if he could move even if he wanted to.

Maladek cursed and groaned and purred as the vibrations from her whimpers and moans shot electricity up his spine. His hips rocked in time with the wet slip of her lips. He threw his head back. The sight of her lust filled expression paired with the heavy cloud of her arousal in the air was too much for any mortal to withstand.

"Love," he tried, but the word came out cracked. His balls were growing tight, the suction of her mouth too divine to ignore any longer. "Drink me down, female." He urged, sinking his fingers into her hair.

She released a whimper at his words, her nails gripping his thighs hard enough to break skin as she sped her pace. Maladek exploded with a strangled roar. Waves of pleasure blinded him as his cock pulsed within the warm cavern of her mouth. She lapped him up eagerly, working her tongue over his sensitive flesh until he had to pull her away.

He panted and just managed to hold her at arm's length as she tried to leap onto his lap. The vishou had taken full effect, the blue of her eyes a mere sliver visible around her enlarged pupils. Blood rushed back to his shaft at the knowledge she'd be slick and ready for him.

Leisurely teasing could wait until another day. His mate needed release, and he refused to withhold it from her. Maladek flipped her to her back and trapped her wriggling hips beneath his hands while he loomed over her.

Katie was glorious under him, her skin flushed, her lips red, and a faint shimmer of sweat glistened on her chest. His gaze met her stiff nipples, and she arched her back toward him, straining to give him access. "Please Maladek," she begged.

"Love, will you ask me?" he urged, running one of his palms up her stomach until it reached her rib cage. She shivered at the touch and let out a frustrated moan. "Ask me like you did in the cave," he pressed.

Her blonde brows furrowed, and her lids slid closed like she was deep in thought, despite her body nearly vibrating with need.

A dazzling smile broke over her face and her eyes flashed open triumphantly when she recalled the words she'd spoken. "Please fuck me, Maladek."

He matched her grin and didn't pull away when she wrenched his face down to hers and kissed him. The head of his cock pressed against her entrance, and his eyes rolled back to feel how slick she was for him. Her body primed, he slid inside in one smooth stroke.

As though her nerves had merely been waiting for the contact, she released a strangled moan, muscles shooting tight. With only a few more rough thrusts, she came apart underneath him.

Maladek remained still until her orgasm had calmed and her breathing evened out. He ran his lips and tongue over her neck, her ear, her jaw, and pumped in and out of her tight sex. Her thin arms and legs wrapped around his body and squeezed as though she longed to feel his full weight press her into the soft cushions.

She came again when he rolled her nipple between his teeth, her palms gripping his horns to keep his mouth working the way she liked.

The rest of the night passed in a blur of sweat, rasping breath, and whispered endearments. He took her against the wall. While bent over a table. Amid tangles of soft bedding. The last time he came, she'd moaned his praises into his ear while he was buried deep inside her.

After some time, he refused to fuck her for fear of making her soreness tomorrow unbearable. Instead, he dipped his tongue between her thighs and rang out gentle orgasms until the vishou left her system.

Though exhausted and bleary eyed, they somehow managed to wash themselves before collapsing into bed together. Pulling energy from his demanding mating bond, he rubbed a salve over Katie's body that would ease any lingering soreness. Then, not strong enough to deny her when she demanded, he let her do the same, grinning like a fool as the female of his fantasies hummed a sweet melody and tended to him.

Epilogue

Five months later

Glittering white blankets of snow covered the mountains as far as Katie could see. She crossed her arms on the ledge of her outdoor hot spring and gazed across the valley. The spring was just outside their bedroom and not only overlooked the Tetranican mountain range but also an enormous waterfall.

Icicles the size of cars dripped down the rock face at the moment, but Maladek had assured her that in the summer the water would cascade over the mountain and create a near constant rainbow in the mist.

Though it sounded magical and she was sure she'd love the sight, Katie already knew that winter would be her favorite season. She'd always taken the beauty and peacefulness of the world after a heavy snowstorm for granted, and only now realized how much she'd missed it.

Maladek emerged from the house fully naked, and Katie couldn't help but ogle him. She'd never tire of the sight of his powerful body or his handsome ruby-eyed gaze. He deftly slid into the pool of water while holding two steaming cups of liquid in his hands.

"For my loves," he rumbled, placing a cup in front of her. She grinned at the new name he'd begun using. Slipping in behind her, he held his beverage with one hand and rested his other protectively over her belly. They'd only found out about the pregnancy a few weeks ago, yet Maladek swore he felt a flutter when he laid his hand over her womb. She didn't mind, even if she didn't believe him. His need to touch her remained constant, child or no, and she wouldn't have it any other way.

She dropped her head against his shoulder and sipped the warm drink.

"What do you think of the first snow?" he whispered into her hair.

"I love it."

Maladek must have heard something in her voice because he lifted her chin, angling it so she peered back at him. "Is there something under your words, my Katie?"

She gave his fingertips a soft kiss. "No, no. I'm fine. I'd like to go out into the snow sometime. That's all." The temperature-controlled bubble of the patio shielded the occupants against the weather and without feeling the cold on her skin, the glistening snow didn't seem real. Like she was watching it on TV or always looking at nature from behind a window, never existing in it. "I'd like to feel the cold again."

"I could remove the environmental controls?" he offered with a raised brow.

She did a double take and the corner of her mouth lifted. "You can turn it off? Why didn't you say anything? I didn't know that."

Maladek shrugged and gave her a sheepish grin. "I didn't think you'd want to remove them. It's frigid out there. Are you sure?"

Katie was nodding before he'd finished his sentence.

Without another word, Maladek hopped out of the warm spring water and sprinted into the house. He emerged holding a screen and pressed a few buttons as he rejoined her in the water. Before he lowered the environment, he wrapped his arms around her shoulders and braced himself.

A blast of bitterly cold air hit her face and stole her breath. Both she and Maladek instinctively ducked into the warm water. Once the shock wore off, Katie braved the icy breeze, setting her mug aside. She sucked in a deep breath, almost coughing from the thin oxygen.

Crisp and fresh, the air burned her lungs in the best way. Sudden emotion welled in her chest. Betuhines was a temperate planet. The palace was never too hot or too cold. Sielijia had been humid and warm.

There was only one other place she could remember weather like this. A place where the sun shone in the electric blue sky and lit up glittering snowflakes in powdery snow. Something about the feeling of an icy breeze making the tips of her ears numb and the indefinable smell of truly cold air brought back flashes of memory. Ice skating in her hometown. Showing her little brother how to form a snowball one happy snow day. Katie and her mother frantically scraping ice off the car in the morning so she wouldn't be late for school.

She swiped a tear away, and found Maladek peering down at her, worry shining in his eyes.

"It reminds me of Earth…the cold." She shot him a watery grin, letting him know her tears were happy ones.

His spine straightened, and he gripped her hand more firmly. "It makes you miss your home planet."

"I think…" Katie had been secretly pondering this since she'd learned she was pregnant, but hadn't worked up the courage to say her thoughts out loud. She hadn't even made her own mind up about anything yet, but the winter and the memories that returned with it decided for her. "If Clecania succeeds in changing Earth's status, I think I'd like to try to find my family." The last of her words were uttered in little more than a whisper. "I'd like you to meet them." She dipped back under the water and floated into Maladek's waiting arms. "And I'd like them to meet our baby."

"I'll do everything in my power to help you." The look on his face was so solemn, as if this would be the most serious assignment of his life.

Katie lifted her hand to his cheek and her gaze caught on the beautiful ring he'd gifted her after learning of her secret longing for a human wedding ring. They'd argued about which of the priceless gems to use, but eventually she'd convinced him that though there were many of a finer quality, the stone she wanted to see on her hand every day meant more to her than any of the others. Now cut and polished, the blue stone he'd gifted her in the Sieliji caves glinted in the sun. Her heart swelled every time she looked at it.

"I want you to know that even though I may have family on Earth and family on Betuhines, I only ever want to be here with you. I used to feel like I'd never belong anywhere. You changed that. You're the only reason I have the strength to think about visiting Earth at all. Because I know you'll be there with me."

Earth, Betuhines, Clecania. My mate who is loved throughout the universe." Maladek tugged at one of her stretched wet curls, his reverent smile matching the tenderness in his eyes. "You have more family than you know, and to me you are everything." With a deep breath, he tucked her against his chest. "You're my whole universe Katie."

About the Author

Victoria Aveline has always enjoyed immersing herself in a good romance. Alpha males are her weakness but, while possessive dominating heroes have always been titillating, she craved something more. So she decided to create a world in which devastatingly sexy men could be aggressive and domineering but still bow down before the matriarchy.

Victoria lives with her husband, dogs, and about sixty thousand badass honey-making ladies. When not writing or fantasizing about future characters, she enjoys traveling, reading, and sipping overpriced hipster cocktails.

www.victoriaaveline.com

www.ingramcontent.com/pod-product-compliance
Lightning Source LLC
Chambersburg PA
CBHW061819190726
48289CB00007B/2256